LAW OF THE DESERT

**Center Point
Large Print**

**This Large Print Book carries the
Seal of Approval of N.A.V.H.**

LAW OF THE DESERT

Western Stories

LOUIS L'AMOUR

edited by
JON TUSKA

A Circle Ⓥ Western

CENTER POINT PUBLISHING
THORNDIKE, MAINE

This Center Point Large Print edition
is published in the year 2007 in cooperation with
Golden West Literary Agency.

First Edition.

The text of this Large Print edition is unabridged. In other
aspects, this book may vary from the original edition. Printed in
Thailand. Set in 16-point Times New Roman type.

ISBN-10: 1-60285-023-2
ISBN-13: 978-1-60285-023-1

Library of Congress Cataloging-in-Publication Data

L'Amour, Louis, 1908-1988.
    Law of the desert / Louis L'Amour.--Center Point large print ed.
    p. cm.
    ISBN-13: 978-1-60285-023-1 (lib. bdg. : alk. paper)
    1. Large type books. I. Title.

PS3523.A446L38 2007
813'.52--dc22

2007010458

Acknowledgments

"The Black Rock Coffin Makers" first appeared in .44 Western (2/50). Copyright © 1950 by Popular Publications, Inc. Copyright not renewed.

"Grub Line Rider" under the byline Jim Mayo first appeared in *Triple Western* (6/51). Copyright © 1951 by Better Publications, Inc. Copyright not renewed.

"Desert Death Song" first appeared in *Dime Western* (2/50). Copyright © 1950 by Popular Publications, Inc. Copyright not renewed.

"One Last Gun Notch" first appeared in *.44 Western* (5/42). Copyright © 1942 by Popular Publications, Inc. Copyright not renewed.

"Ride, You Tonto Raiders" first appeared in *New Western* (8/49). Copyright © 1949 by Popular Publications, Inc. Copyright not renewed.

"War Party" first appeared in *The Saturday Evening Post* (6/13/59). Copyright © 1959 by The Curtis Publishing Company. Copyright © renewed 1987 by The Curtis Publishing Company. Reprinted by permission of The Curtis Publishing Company.

"Law of the Desert" first appeared under the title "Law of the Desert Born" in *Dime Western* (4/46). Copyright © 1946 by Popular Publications, Inc. Copyright not renewed.

TABLE OF CONTENTS

LAW OF THE DESERT

Introduction
by Jon Tuska

Louis Dearborn LaMoore (1908-1988) was born in Jamestown, North Dakota. He left home at fifteen and subsequently held a wide variety of jobs although he worked mostly as a merchant seaman. From his earliest youth, L'Amour had a love of verse. His first published work was a poem, "The Chap Worth While", appearing when he was eighteen years old in his former hometown's newspaper, the *Jamestown Sun*. It is the only poem from his early years that he left out of "Smoke from this Altar" which appeared in 1939 from Lusk Publishers in Oklahoma City, a book which L'Amour published himself; however, this poem is reproduced in *The Louis L'Amour Companion* (Andrews and McMeel, 1992) edited by Robert Weinberg. L'Amour wrote poems and articles for a number of small circulation arts magazines all through the early 1930s and, after hundreds of rejection slips, finally had his first story accepted, "Anything for a Pal" in *True Gang Life* (10/35). He returned in 1938 to live with his family where they had settled in Choctaw, Oklahoma, determined to make writing his career. He wrote a fight story bought by Standard Magazines that year and became acquainted with editor Leo Margulies who was to play an important rôle later in L'Amour's life. "The Town No Guns Could Tame" in *New Western*

11

(3/40) was his first published Western story.

During the Second World War L'Amour was drafted and ultimately served with the U.S. Army Transportation Corps in Europe. However, in the two years before he was shipped out, he managed to write a great many adventure stories for Standard Magazines. The first story he published in 1946, the year of his discharge, was a Western, "Law of the Desert Born" in *Dime Western* (4/46). A call to Leo Margulies resulted in L'Amour's agreeing to write Western stories for the various Western pulp magazines published by Standard Magazines, a third of which appeared under the byline Jim Mayo, the name of a character in L'Amour's earlier adventure fiction. The proposal for L'Amour to write new Hopalong Cassidy novels came from Margulies who wanted to launch *Hopalong Cassidy's Western Magazine* to take advantage of the popularity William Boyd's old films and new television series were enjoying with a new generation. Doubleday & Company agreed to publish the pulp novelettes in hard cover books. L'Amour was paid $500 a story, no royalties, and he was assigned the house name Tex Burns. L'Amour read Clarence E. Mulford's books about the Bar-20 and based his Hopalong Cassidy on Mulford's original creation. Only two issues of the magazine appeared before it ceased publication. Doubleday felt that the Hopalong character had to appear exactly as William Boyd did in the films and on television and thus even the first two novels had to be revamped to meet with this requirement prior to publication in book form.

L'Amour's first Western novel under his own byline was *Westward the Tide* (World's Work, 1950). It was rejected by every American publisher to which it was submitted. World's Work paid a flat £75 without royalties for British Empire rights in perpetuity. L'Amour sold his first Western short story to a slick magazine a year later, "The Gift of Cochise" in *Collier's* (7/5/52). Robert Fellows and John Wayne purchased screen rights to this story from L'Amour for $4,000 and James Edward Grant, one of Wayne's favorite screenwriters, developed a script from it, changing L'Amour's Ches Lane to Hondo Lane. L'Amour retained the right to novelize Grant's screenplay, which differs substantially from his short story, and he was able to get an endorsement from Wayne to be used as a blurb, stating that *Hondo* was the finest Western Wayne had ever read. *Hondo* (Fawcett Gold Medal, 1953) by Louis L'Amour was released on the same day as the film, *Hondo* (Warner, 1953), with a first printing of 320,000 copies.

With *Showdown at Yellow Butte* (Ace, 1953) by Jim Mayo, L'Amour began a series of short Western novels for Don Wollheim that could be doubled with other short novels by other authors in Ace Publishing's paperback two-fers. Advances on these were $800 and usually the author never earned any royalties. *Heller with a Gun* (Fawcett Gold Medal, 1955) was the first of a series of original Westerns

L'Amour had agreed to write under his own name following the success for Fawcett of *Hondo*. L'Amour wanted even this early to have his Western novels published in hard cover editions. He expanded "Guns of the Timberland" by Jim Mayo in *West* (9/50) for *Guns of the Timberlands* (Jason Press, 1955), a hard cover Western for which he was paid an advance of $250. Another novel for Jason Press followed and then *Silver Cañon* (Avalon Books, 1956) for Thomas Bouregy & Company. These were basically lending library publishers and the books seldom earned much money above the small advances paid.

The great turn in L'Amour's fortunes came about because of problems Saul David was having with his original paperback Westerns program at Bantam Books. Fred Glidden had been signed to a contract to produce two original paperback Luke Short Western novels a year for an advance of $15,000 each. It was a long-term contract but, in the first ten years of it, Fred only wrote six novels. Literary agent Marguerite Harper then persuaded Bantam that Fred's brother, Jon, could help fulfill the contract and Jon was signed for eight Peter Dawson Western novels. When Jon died suddenly before completing even one book for Bantam, Harper managed to engage a ghost writer at the Disney studios to write these eight "Peter Dawson" novels, beginning with *The Savages* (Bantam, 1959). They proved inferior to anything Jon had ever written and what sales they had seemed to be due only to the Peter Dawson name.

Saul David wanted to know from L'Amour if *he* could deliver two Western novels a year. L'Amour said he could, and he did. In fact, by 1962 this number was increased to three original paperback novels a year. The first L'Amour novel to appear under the Bantam contract was *Radigan* (Bantam, 1958). It seemed to me after I read all of the Western stories L'Amour ever wrote in preparation for my essay, "Louis L'Amour's Western Fiction" in *A Variable Harvest* (McFarland, 1990), that by the time L'Amour wrote "Riders of the Dawn" in *Giant Western* (6/51), the short novel he later expanded to form *Silver Cañon*, that he had almost burned out on the Western story, and this was years before his fame, wealth, and tremendous sales figures. He had developed seven basic plot situations in his pulp Western stories and he used them over and over again in writing his original paperback Westerns. *Flint* (Bantam, 1960), considered by many to be one of L'Amour's better efforts, is basically a reprise of the range war plot which, of the seven, is the one L'Amour used most often. L'Amour's hero, Flint, knows about a hide-out in the badlands (where, depending on the story, something is hidden: cattle, horses, outlaws, etc.). Even certain episodes within his basic plots are repeated again and again. Flint scales a sharp V in a cañon wall to escape a tight spot as Jim Gatlin had before him in L'Amour's "The Black Rock Coffin Makers" in *.44 Western* (2/50) and many a L'Amour hero would again.

Basic to this range war plot is the villain's means for crowding out the other ranchers in a district. He brings in a giant herd that requires all the available grass and forces all the smaller ranchers out of business. It was this same strategy Bantam used in marketing L'Amour. *All* of his Western titles were continuously kept in print. Independent distributors were required to buy titles in lots of 10,000 copies if they wanted access to other Bantam titles at significantly discounted prices. In time L'Amour's paperbacks forced almost every one else off the racks in the Western sections. L'Amour himself comprised the other half of this successful strategy. He dressed up in cowboy outfits, traveled about the country in a motor home visiting with independent distributors, taking them to dinner and charming them, making them personal friends. He promoted himself at every available opportunity. L'Amour insisted that he was telling the stories of the people who had made America a great nation and he appealed to patriotism as much as to commercialism in his rhetoric.

His fiction suffered, of course, stories written hurriedly and submitted in their first draft and published as he wrote them. A character would have a rifle in his hand, a model not yet invented in the period in which the story was set, and when he crossed a street the rifle would vanish without explanation. A scene would begin in a saloon and suddenly the setting would be a hotel dining room. Characters would die once and, a few pages later, die again. An old man for most of a story would turn out to be in his twenties.

Once when we were talking and Louis had showed me his topographical maps and his library of thousands of volumes which he claimed he used for research, he asserted that, if he claimed there was a rock in a road at a certain point in a story, his readers knew that if they went to that spot they would find the rock just as he described it. I told him that might be so but I personally was troubled by the many inconsistencies in his stories. Take *Last Stand at Papago Wells* (Fawcett Gold Medal, 1957). Five characters are killed during an Indian raid. One of the surviving characters emerges from seclusion after the attack and counts *six* corpses.

"I'll have to go back and count them again," L'Amour said, and smiled. "But, you know, I don't think the people who read my books would really care."

All of this notwithstanding, there are many fine, and some spectacular, moments in Louis L'Amour's Western fiction. I think he was at his best in the shorter forms, especially his magazine stories, and the two best stories he ever wrote appeared in the 1950s, "The Gift of Cochise" early in the decade and "War Party" in *The Saturday Evening Post* (6/59). The latter was later expanded by L'Amour to serve as the opening chapters for *Bendigo Shafter* (Dutton, 1979). That book is so poorly structured that Harold

Kuebler, senior editor at Doubleday & Company to whom it was first offered, said he would not publish it unless L'Amour undertook extensive revisions. This L'Amour refused to do and, eventually, Bantam started a hard cover publishing program to accommodate him when no other hard cover publisher proved willing to accept his books as he wrote them. Yet "War Party," reprinted here as it first appeared, possesses several of the characteristics in purest form which I suspect, no matter how diluted they ultimately would become, account in largest measure for the loyal following Louis L'Amour won from his readers: the young male narrator who is in the process of growing into manhood and who is evaluating other human beings and his own experiences; a resourceful frontier woman who has beauty as well as fortitude; a strong male character who is single and hence marriageable; and the powerful, romantic, strangely compelling vision of the American West which invests L'Amour's Western fiction and makes it such a delightful escape from the cares of a later time — in this author's words from this story, that "big country needing big men and women to live in it" and where there was no place for "the frightened or the mean."

The Black Rock Coffin Makers

I

Jim Gatlin had been up the creek and over the mountains, and more than once had been on both ends of a six-shooter. Lean and tall, with shoulders wide for his height and a face like saddle leather, he was, at the moment, doing a workman-like job of demolishing the last of a thick steak and picking off isolated beans that had escaped his initial attack. He was 1,000 miles from home and knew nobody in the town of Tucker.

He glanced up as the door opened and saw a short, thick-bodied man. The man gave one startled look at Jim and ducked back out of sight. Gatlin blinked in surprise, then shrugged and filled his coffee cup from the pot standing on the restaurant table.

Puzzled, he listened to the rapidly receding pound of a horse's hoofs, then rolled a smoke, sitting back with a contented sigh. Some 250-odd miles to the north was the herd he had drifted northwest from Texas. The money the cattle had brought was in the belt around his waist and his pants pockets. Nothing remained now but to return to Texas, bank the profit, and pick up a new herd.

The outer door opened again, and a tall girl entered the restaurant. Turning right, she started for the door leading to the hotel. She stopped abruptly as though his presence had only then registered. She turned, and her eyes widened in alarm. Swiftly she crossed the room to him.

"Are you insane?" she whispered. "Sitting here like that when the town is full of Wing Cary's hands? They know you're coming and have been watching for you for days."

Gatlin looked up, smiling. "Ma'am, you've sure got the wrong man, although if a girl as pretty as you is worried about him, he sure is a lucky fellow. I'm a stranger here. I never saw the place until an hour ago."

She stepped back, puzzled, and then the door slammed open once more, and a man stepped into the room. He was as tall as Jim, but thinner, and his dark eyes were angry. "Get away from him, Lisa! I'm killin' him . . . right now!"

The man's hand flashed for a gun, and Gatlin dived sidewise to the floor, drawing as he fell. A gun roared in the room, then Gatlin fired twice.

The tall man caught himself, jerking his left arm against his ribs, his face twisted as he gasped for breath. Then he wilted slowly to the floor, his gun sliding from his fingers.

Gatlin got to his feet, staring at the stranger. He swung his eyes to the girl staring at him. "Who is that *hombre?*" he snapped. "What's this all about? Who did he think I was?"

"You . . . you're not . . . you aren't Jim Walker?" Her voice was high, amazed.

20

"Walker?" He shook his head. "I'm sure as hell not. The name is Gatlin. I'm just driftin' through."

There was a rush of feet in the street outside. She caught his hand. "Come. Come quickly. They won't listen to you. They'll kill you. All the Cary outfit are in town."

She ran beside him, dodging into the hotel, and then swiftly down a hall. As the front door burst open, they plunged out the back and into the alley behind the building. Unerringly she led him to the left, and then opened the back door of another building and drew him inside. Silently she closed the door and stood closely beside him, panting in the darkness.

Shouts and curses rang from the building next door. A door *banged*, and men charged up and down outside. Jim was still holding his gun, but now he withdrew the empty shells and fed two into the cylinder to replace those fired. He slipped a sixth into the usually empty chamber. "What is this place?" he whispered. "Will they come here?"

"It's a law office," she whispered. "I work here part time, and I left the door open myself. They'll not think of this place." Stealthily she lifted the bar and dropped it into place. "Better sit down. They'll be searching the streets for some time."

He found the desk and seated himself on the corner, well out of line with the windows. He could see only the vaguest outline of her face. His first impression of moments before was strong enough for

21

him to remember she was pretty. The gray eyes were wide and clear, her figure rounded yet slim. "What is this?" he repeated. "What was he gunnin' for me for?"

"It wasn't you. He thought you were Jim Walker of the XY. If you aren't actually him, you look enough like him to be a brother, a twin brother."

"Where is he? What goes on here? Who was that *hombre* who tried to gun me down?"

She paused, and seemed to be thinking, and he had the idea she was still uncertain whether to believe him or not. "The man you killed was Bill Trout. He was the badman of Paradise country and *segundo* on Wing Cary's Flying C spread. Jim Walker called him a thief and a murderer in talking to Cary, and Trout threatened to shoot him on sight. Walker hasn't been seen since, and that was four days ago, so everybody believed Walker had skipped the country. Nobody blamed him much."

"What's it all about?" Gatlin inquired.

"North of here, up beyond Black Rock, is Alder Creek country, with some rich bottom hay land lying in several corners of the mountains. This is dry country, but that Alder Creek area has springs and some small streams flowing down out of the hills. The streams flow into the desert and die there, so the water is good only for the man who controls the range."

"And that was Walker?"

"No, up until three weeks ago, it was old Dave

22

Butler. Then Dave was thrown from his horse and killed, and, when they read his will, he had left the property to be sold at auction and the money to be paid to his nephew and niece back in New York. However, the joker was, he stipulated that Jim Walker was to get the ranch if he would bid ten thousand cash and forty thousand on his note, payable in six years."

"In other words, he wanted Walker to have the property?" Jim asked. "He got first chance at it?"

"That's right. And I was to get second chance. If Jim didn't want to make the bid, I could have it for the same price. If neither of us wanted it, the ranch was to go on public auction, and that means that Cary and Horwick would get it. They have the money, and nobody around here could outbid them."

The street outside was growing quieter as the excitement of the chase died down. "I think," Lisa continued, "that Uncle Dave wanted Jim to have the property because Jim did so much to develop it. Jim was foreman of the XY acting for Dave. Then, Uncle Dave knew my father and liked me, and he knew I loved the ranch, so he wanted me to have second chance, but I don't have the money, and they all know it. Jim had some of it, and he could get the rest. I think that was the real issue behind his trouble with Trout. I believe Wing deliberately set Trout to kill him, and Jim's statements about Bill were a result of the pushing around Bill Trout had given him."

The pattern was not unfamiliar, and Gatlin could

easily appreciate the situation. Water was gold in this country of sparse grass. To a cattleman, such a ranch as Lisa described could be second to none, with plenty of water and grass and good hay meadows. Suddenly she caught his arm. Men were talking outside the door.

"Looks like he got plumb away, Wing. Old Ben swears there was nobody in the room with him but that Lisa Cochrane, an' she never threw that gun, but how Jim Walker ever beat Trout is more'n I can see. Why, Bill was the fastest man around here unless it's you or me."

"That wasn't Walker, Pete. It couldn't have been."

"Ben swears it was, an' Woody Hammer busted right through the door in front of him. Said it was Jim, all right."

Wing Cary's voice was irritable. "I tell you, it couldn't have been!" he flared. "Jim Walker never saw the day he dared face Trout with a gun. I've seen Walker draw an' he never was fast."

"Maybe he wasn't," Pete Chasin agreed dryly, "but Trout's dead, ain't he?"

"Three days left," Cary said. "Lisa Cochrane hasn't the money, and it doesn't look like Walker will even be bidding. Let it ride, Pete. I don't think we need to worry about anything. Even if that was Walker . . . an' I'd take an oath it wasn't . . . he's gone for good now. All we have to do is sit tight."

The two moved off, and Jim Gatlin, staring at the girl in the semidarkness, saw her lips were tightly pressed. His eyes had grown accustomed to the dim light, and he could see around the small office. It was a simple room with a desk, chair, and filing cabinets. Well-filled bookcases lined the walls.

He got to his feet. "I've got to get my gear out of that hotel," he said, "and my horse."

"You're leaving?" she asked.

Jim glanced at her in surprise. "Why, sure. Why stay here in a fight that's not my own? I've already killed one man, and, if I stay, I'll have to kill more or be killed myself. There's nothing here for me."

"Did you notice something?" she asked suddenly. "Wing Cary seemed very sure that Jim Walker wasn't coming back, that you weren't he."

Gatlin frowned. He had noticed it, and it had him wondering. "He did sound mighty sure. Like he might know Walker wasn't coming back."

They were silent in the dark office, yet each knew what the other was thinking. Jim Walker was dead. Pete Chasin had not known it. Neither, obviously, had Bill Trout.

"What happens to you then?" Gatlin asked suddenly. "You lose the ranch?"

She shrugged. "I never had it, and never really thought I would have it, only . . . well, if Jim had lived . . . I mean, if Jim got the ranch, we'd have made out. We were very close, like brother and sister. Now I don't know what I can do."

"You haven't any people?"

"None that I know of." Her head came up sud-

25

denly. "Oh, it isn't myself I'm thinking of, it's all the old hands, the ranch itself. Uncle Dave hated Cary, and so do his men. Now he'll get the ranch, and they'll all be fired, and he'll ruin the place. That's what he's wanted all along."

Gatlin shifted his feet. "Tough," he said, "mighty tough." He opened the door slightly. "Thanks," he said, "for getting me out of there."

She didn't reply, so, after a moment, he stepped out of the door and drew it gently to behind him.

There was no time to lose. He must be out of town by daylight and with miles behind him. There was no sense getting mixed up in somebody else's fight, for all he'd get out of it would be a bellyful of lead. There was nothing he could do to help. He moved swiftly, and within a matter of minutes was in his hotel room. Apparently searching for Jim Walker, they hadn't considered his room in the hotel, so Gatlin got his duffel together, stuffed it into his saddlebags, and picked up his rifle. With utmost care, he eased down the back stairs and into the alley.

The streets were once more dark and still. What had become of the Flying C hands he didn't know, but none was visible. Staying on back streets, he made his way carefully to the livery barn, but there his chance of cover grew less, for he must enter the wide door with a light glowing over it.

After listening, he stepped out and, head down, walked through the door. Turning, he hurried to the stall where his powerful black waited. It was the work of only a few minutes to saddle up. He led the horse out of the stall and caught up the bridle. As his hand grasped the pommel, a voice stopped him.

"Lightin' out?"

It was Pete Chasin's voice. Slowly he released his grip on the pommel and turned slightly. The man was hidden in a stall.

"Why not?" Gatlin asked. "I'm not goin' to be a shootin' gallery for nobody. This ain't my range, an' I'm slopin' out of here for Texas. I'm no trouble hunter."

He heard Chasin's chuckle. "Don't reckon you are. But it seems a shame not to make the most of your chance. What if I offered you five thousand to stay? Five thousand, in cash?"

"Five thousand?" Gatlin blinked. That was half as much as he had in his belt, and the $10,000 he carried had taken much hard work and bargaining to get. Buying a herd, chancing the long drive.

"What would I have to do?" he demanded.

Chasin came out of the stall. "Be yourself," he said, "just be yourself . . . but let folks think you're Jim Walker. Then you buy a ranch here . . . I'll give you the money, an' then you hit the trail."

Chasin was trying to double-cross Cary? To get the ranch for himself?

Gatlin hesitated. "That's a lot of money, but these boys toss a lot of lead. I might not live to spend the dough."

"I'll hide you out," Chasin argued. "I've got a

27

cabin in the hills. I'd hide you out with four or five of my boys to stand guard. You'd be safe enough. Then you could come down, put your money on the line, an' sign the papers."

"Suppose they want Walker's signature checked?"

"Jim Walker never signed more'n three, four papers in his life. He left no signatures hereabouts. I've took pains to be sure."

$5,000 because he looked like a man. It was easy money, and he'd be throwing a monkey wrench into Wing Cary's plans. Cary, a man he'd decided he disliked. "Sounds like a deal," he said. "Let's go!"

The cabin on the north slope of Bartlett Peak was well hidden, and there was plenty of grub. Pete Chasin left him there with two men to guard him and two more standing by on the trail toward town. All through the following day, Jim Gatlin loafed, smoking cigarettes and talking idly with the two men. Hab Johnson was a big, unshaven *hombre* with a sullen face and a surly manner. He talked little, and then only to growl. Pink Stabineau was a wide-chested, flat-faced jasper with an agreeable grin.

Gatlin had a clear idea of his own situation. He could use $5,000, but he knew Chasin never intended him to leave the country with it and doubted if he would last an hour after the ranch was transferred to Chasin himself. Yet Gatlin had been around the rough country, and he knew a trick or two of his own. Several times he thought of Lisa Cochrane, but avoided that angle as much as he could.

After all, she had no chance to get the ranch, and Walker was probably dead. That left it between Cary and Chasin. The unknown Horwick, of whom he had heard mention, was around, too, but he seemed to stand with Cary in everything.

Yet Gatlin was restless and irritable, and he kept remembering the girl beside him in the darkness and her regrets at breaking up the old outfit. Jim Gatlin had been a hand who rode for the brand; he knew what it meant to have a ranch sold out from under a bunch of old hands. The home that had been theirs gone, the friends drifting apart never to meet again, everything changed.

He finished breakfast on the morning of the second day, then walked out of the cabin with his saddle. Hab Johnson looked up sharply. "Where you goin'?" he demanded.

"Ridin'," Gatlin said briefly, "an' don't worry. I'll be back."

Johnson chewed a stem of grass, his hard eyes on Jim's. "You ain't goin' nowheres. The boss said to watch you an' keep you here. Here you stay."

Gatlin dropped his saddle. "You aren't keepin' me nowhere, Hab," he said flatly. "I've had enough sittin' around. I aim to see a little of this country."

"I reckon not." Hab got to his feet. "You may be a fast hand with a gun, but you ain't gittin' both of us, and you ain't so foolish as to try." He waved a big hand. "Now you go back an' set down."

"I started for a ride," Jim said quietly, "and a ride

I'm takin'." He stooped to pick up the saddle and saw Hab's boots as the big man started for him. Jim had lifted the saddle clear of the ground, and now he hurled it, suddenly, in Hab's path. The big man stumbled and hit the ground on his hands and knees, then started up.

As he came up halfway, Jim slugged him. Hab tottered, fighting for balance, and Gatlin moved in, striking swiftly with a volley of lefts and rights to the head. Hab went down and hit hard, then came up with a lunge, but Gatlin dropped him again. Blood dripped from smashed lips and a cut on his cheek bone.

Gatlin stepped back, working his fingers. His hard eyes flicked to Pink Stabineau, who was smoking quietly, resting on one elbow, looking faintly amused. "You stoppin' me?" Gatlin demanded.

Pink grinned. "Me? Now where did you get an idea like that? Take your ride. Hab's just too persnickety about things. Anyway, he's always wantin' to slug somebody. Now maybe he'll be quiet for a spell."

There was a dim trail running northwest from the cabin and Gatlin took it, letting his horse choose his own gait. The black was a powerful animal, not only good on a trail but an excellent roping horse, and he moved out eagerly, liking the new country. When Gatlin had gone scarcely more than two miles, he skirted the edge of a high meadow with plenty of grass, then left the trail and turned off along a bench of the mountain, riding due north.

Suddenly the mountain fell away before him, and below, in a long finger of grass, he saw the silver line of a creek, and nestled against a shoulder of the mountain he discerned roofs among the trees. Pausing, Jim rolled a smoke and studied the lay of the land. Northward, for all of ten miles, there was good range. Dry, but not so bad as over the mountain, and in the spring and early summer it would be good grazing land. He had looked at too much range not to detect from the colors of the valley before him some of the varieties of grass and brush. Northwest, the range stretched away through a wide gap in the mountains, and he seemed to distinguish a deeper green in the distance.

Old Dave Butler had chosen well, and his XY had been well handled, Gatlin could see as he rode nearer. Tanks had been built to catch some of the overflow from the mountains and to prevent the washing away of valuable range. The old man, and evidently Jim Walker, had worked hard to build this ranch into something. Even while wanting money for his relatives in the East, Butler had tried to ensure that the work would be continued after his death. Walker would continue it, and so would Lisa Cochrane.

II

All morning he rode, and well into the afternoon, studying the range but avoiding the buildings. Once, glancing back, he saw a group of horsemen riding swiftly out of the mountains from which he had come and heading for the XY. Reining in, he watched from a vantage point among some huge boulders. Men wouldn't ride that fast without adequate reason.

Morosely he turned and started back along the way he had come, thinking more and more of Lisa. $5,000 was a lot of money, but what he was doing was not dishonest, and so far he had played the game straight. Still, why think of that? In a few days, he'd have the money in his pocket and be headed for Texas. He turned on the brow of the hill and glanced back, carried away despite himself by the beauty of the wide sweep of range.

Pushing on, he skirted around and came toward the cabin where he had been staying, off from the town trail. He was riding with his mind far away when the black snorted violently and shied. Jim drew up, staring at the man who lay sprawled in the trail. It was the cowhand Pete Chasin had left on guard there. He'd been shot through the stomach, and a horse had been ridden over him.

Swinging down, a quick check showed that the man was dead. Jim grabbed up the reins and sprang into the saddle. Sliding a six-gun from its holster, he pushed forward, riding cautiously. The tracks told him that a party of twelve horsemen had come this way.

He heard the wind in the trees, the distant cry of an eagle, but nothing more. He rode out into the clearing before the cabin, and drew up. Another man had died here. It wasn't Stabineau or Hab Johnson, but the other guard, who must have retreated to this point for aid.

Gun in hand, Gatlin pushed the door open and looked into the cabin. Everything was smashed, yet when he swung down and went in, he found his own gear intact, under the overturned bed. He threw his bedroll on his horse and loaded up his saddlebags. He jacked a shell into the chamber of the Winchester and was about to mount up when he heard a muffled cry.

Turning, he stared around, then detected a faint stir among the leaves of a mountain mahogany. Warily he walked over and stepped around the bush.

Pink Stabineau, his face pale and his shirt dark with blood, lay sprawled on the ground. Curiously there was still a faint touch of humor in his eyes when he looked up at Gatlin. "Got me," he said finally. "It was that damned Hab. He sold us out . . . to Wing Cary. The damn' dirty . . . !"

Jim dropped to his knees and gently unbuttoned the man's shirt. The wound was low down on the left side, and, although he seemed to have lost much

33

blood, there was a chance. Working swiftly, he built a fire, heated water, and bathed, and then dressed the wound. From time to time, Pink talked, telling him much of what he suspected, that Cary would hunt Chasin down now and kill him.

"If they fight," Jim asked, "who'll win?"

Stabineau grinned wryly. "Cary . . . he's tough, an' cold as ice. Pete's too jumpy. He's fast, but, mark my words, if they face each other, he'll shoot too fast and miss his first shot. Wing won't miss. But it won't come to that. Wing's a cinch player. He'll chase him down an' the bunch will gun him to death. Wing's bloodthirsty."

Leaving food and a canteen of water beside the wounded man and giving him two blankets, Jim Gatlin mounted. His deal was off then. The thought left him with a distinct feeling of relief. He had never liked any part of it, and he found himself without sympathy for Pete Chasin. The man had attempted a double-cross and failed.

Well, the road was open again now, and there was nothing between him and Texas but the miles. Yet he hesitated, and then turned his horse toward the XY. He rode swiftly, and at sundown was at the ranch. He watched it for a time, and saw several hands working around, yet there seemed little activity. No doubt they were waiting to see what was to happen.

Suddenly a sorrel horse started out from the ranch and swung into the trail toward town. Jim Gatlin squinted his eyes against the fading glare of the sun and saw the rider was a woman. That would be Lisa Cochrane.

Suddenly he swung the black and, touching spurs to the horse, raced down the mountain to intercept her.

Until that moment, he had been uncertain as to the proper course, but now he knew. Yet for all his speed, his eyes were alert and watchful, for he realized the risk he ran. Wing Cary would be quick to discover that as long as he was around and alive, there was danger, and even now the rancher might have his men out, scouring the country for him. Certainly there were plausible reasons enough, for it could be claimed that he had joined with Chasin in a plot to get the ranch by pretending to be Jim Walker.

Lisa's eyes widened when she saw him. "I thought you'd be gone by now. There's a posse after you."

"You mean some of Cary's men?" he corrected.

"I mean a posse. Wing has men on your trail, too, but they lost you somehow. He claims that you were tied up in a plan with Pete Chasin to get the ranch, and that you killed Jim Walker."

His eyes searched her face. "You mean he actually claims that?"

She nodded, watching him. "He says that story about your being here was all nonsense, that you actually came on purpose, that you and Chasin rigged it that way. You'll have to admit it looks funny, you arriving right at this time and looking just like Jim."

"What if it does?" he demanded impatiently. "I never heard of Jim Walker until you mentioned him to me, and I never heard of the town of Tucker until a few hours before I met you."

"You'd best go, then," she warned. "They're all over the country. Sheriff Eaton would take you in, but Wing wouldn't, nor any of his boys. They'll kill you on sight."

"Yeah," he agreed. "I can see that." Nevertheless, he didn't stir, but continued to roll a cigarette. She sat still, watching him curiously. Finally he looked up. "I'm in a fight," he admitted, "and not one I asked for. Cary is making this a mighty personal thing, ma'am, an' I reckon I ain't even figurin' on leavin'." He struck a match. "You got any chance of gettin' the ranch?"

"How could I? I have no money!"

"Supposin'," he suggested, squinting an eye against the smoke, "you had a pardner . . . with ten thousand dollars?"

Lisa shook her head. "Things like that don't happen," she said. "They just don't."

"I've got ten thousand dollars on me," Gatlin volunteered, "an' I've been pushed into this whether I like it or not. I say we ride into Tucker now an' we see this boss of yours, the lawyer. I figure he could get the deal all set up for us tomorrow. Are you game?"

"You . . . you really have that much?" She looked doubtfully at his shabby range clothes. "It's honest money?"

36

"I drove cattle to Montana," he said. "That was my piece of it. Let's go."

"Not so fast!" The words rapped out sharply. "I'll take that money, an' take it now! Woody, get that girl!"

For reply Jim slapped the spurs to the black and, at the same instant, slapped the sorrel a ringing blow. The horses sprang off together in a dead run. Behind them, a rifle shot rang out, and Jim felt the bullet clip past his skull. "Keep goin'!" he yelled. "Ride!"

At a dead run, they swung down the trail, and then Jim saw a side trail he had noticed on his left. He jerked his head at the girl and grabbed at her bridle. It was too dark to see the gesture, but she felt the tug and turned the sorrel after him, mounting swiftly up the steep side hill under the trees. There the soft needles made it impossible for their horses' hoofs to be heard, and Jim led the way, pushing on under the pines.

That it would be only a minute or so before Cary discovered his error was certain, but each minute counted. A wall lifted on their right, and they rode on, keeping in the intense darkness close under it, but then another wall appeared on their left, and they were boxed in. Behind them they heard a yell, distant now, but indication enough their trail had been found. Boulders and slabs of rock loomed before them, but the black horse turned down a slight incline and worked his way around the rocks. From time to time, they spoke to each other to keep

37

together, but he kept moving, knowing that Wing Cary would be close behind.

The cañon walls seemed to be drawing closer, and the boulders grew larger and larger. Somewhere Jim heard water running, and the night air was cool and slightly damp on his face. He could smell pine, so he knew that there were trees about and they had not ridden completely out of them. Yet Jim was becoming worried, for the cañon walls towered above them, and obviously there was no break. If this turned out to be a box cañon, they were bottled up. One man could hold this cañon corked with no trouble at all.

The black began to climb and in a few minutes walked out on a flat of grassy land. The moon was rising, but as yet there was no light in this deep cañon.

Lisa rode up beside him. "Jim"—it was the first time she had ever called him by name—"I'm afraid we're in for it now. Unless I'm mistaken, this is a box cañon. I've never been up here, but I've heard of it, and there's no way out."

"I was afraid of that." The black horse stopped as he spoke, and he heard water falling ahead. He urged the horse forward, but he refused to obey. Jim swung down into the darkness. "Pool," he said. "We'll find some place to hole up and wait for daylight."

They found a group of boulders and seated themselves among them, stripping the saddles from their horses and picketing them on a small patch of grass behind the boulders. Then, for a long time, they talked, the casual talk of two people finding out about each other. Jim talked of his early life on the Neuces, of his first trip into Mexico after horses when he was fourteen, and how they were attacked by Apaches. There had been three Indian fights that trip, two south of the border and one north of it.

He had no idea when sleep took him, but he awakened with a start to find the sky growing gray and to see Lisa Cochrane sleeping on the grass six feet away. She looked strangely young, with her face relaxed and her lips slightly parted. A dark tendril of hair had blown across her cheek. He turned away and walked out to the horses. The grass was thick and rich there.

He studied their position with care and found they were on a terrace separated from the end wall of the cañon only by the pool, at least an acre of clear, cold water into which a small fall poured from the cliff above. There were a few trees, and some of the scattered boulders they had encountered the previous night. The cañon on which they had come was a wild jumble of boulders and brush surmounted on either side by cliffs that lifted nearly 300 feet. While escape might be impossible if Wing Cary attempted, as he surely would, to guard the opening, their own position was secure, too, for one man with a rifle might stand off an army from the terrace.

After he had watered the horses, he built a fire and put water on for coffee. Seeing some trout in the pool, he tried his luck, and from the enthusiasm with which they went for his bait, the pool could never have been fished before, or not in a long time.

Lisa came from behind the boulders just as the coffee came to a boil. "What is this? A picnic?" she asked brightly.

He grinned, touching his unshaven jaw. "With this beard?" He studied her a minute. "You'd never guess you'd spent the night on horseback or sleeping at the end of a cañon," he said. Then his eyes sobered. "Can you handle a rifle? I mean, well enough to stand off Cary's boys if they tried to come up here?"

She turned quickly and glanced down the cañon. The nearest boulders to the terrace edge were sixty yards away, and the approach even that close would not be easy. "I think so," she said. "What are you thinking of?"

He gestured at the cliff. "I've been studyin' that. With a mite of luck, a man might make it up there."

Her face paled. "It isn't worth it. We're whipped, and we might as well admit it. All we can do now is sit still and wait until the ranch is sold."

"No," he said positively. "I'm goin' out of here if I have to blast my way out. They've made a personal matter out of this, now, and"—he glanced at her—"I sort of have a feeling you should have that ranch. Lookin' at it yesterday, I just couldn't imagine it without you. You lived there, didn't you?"

"Most of my life. My folks were friends of Uncle

40

Dave's, and after they were killed, I stayed on with him."

"Did he leave you anything?" he asked.

She shook her head. "I . . . I think he expected me to marry Jim. . . . He always wanted it that way, but we never felt like that about each other, and yet Jim told me after Uncle Dave died that I was to consider the place my home, if he got it."

As they ate, he listened to her talk while he studied the cliff. It wasn't going to be easy, and yet it could be done.

A shout rang out from the rocks behind them, and they both moved to the boulders, but there was nobody in sight. A voice yelled again that Jim spotted as that of Wing Cary. He shouted a reply, and Wing yelled back: "We'll let Lisa come out if she wants, an' you, too, if you come with your hands up!"

Lisa shook her head, so Gatlin shouted back, "We like it here! Plenty of water, plenty of grub! If you want us, you'll have to come an' get us!"

In the silence that followed, Lisa said: "He can't stay, not if he attends the auction."

Jim turned swiftly. "Take the rifle. If they start to come, shoot an' shoot to kill. I'm going to take a chance."

Keeping out of sight behind the worn gray boulders, Gatlin worked his way swiftly along the edge of the pool toward the cliff face. As he felt his way along the rocky edge, he stared down into the water.

41

That pool was deep, from the looks of it. And that was something to remember.

At the cliff face, he stared up. It looked even easier than he thought, and at one time and another he had climbed worse faces. However, once he was well up the face, he would be within sight of the watchers below—or would he?

III

He put a hand up and started working his way to a four-inch ledge that projected from the face of the rock and slanted sharply upward. There were occasional clumps of brush growing from the rock, and they would offer some security. A rifle shot rang out behind him, then a half dozen more, farther off. Lisa had fired at something and had been answered from down the cañon.

The ledge was steep, but there were good handholds, and he worked his way along it more swiftly than he would have believed possible. His clothing blended well with the rock, and by refraining from any sudden movements there was a chance that he could make it.

When almost 200 feet up the face, he paused, resting on a narrow ledge, partly concealed by an outcropping. He looked up, but the wall was sheer. Beyond, there was a chimney, but almost too wide for climbing, and the walls looked slick as a blue clay side hill. Yet study the cliff as he would, he could see no other point where he might climb farther. Worse, part of that chimney was exposed to fire from below.

If they saw him, he was through. He'd be stuck, with no chance of evading their fire. Yet he knew he'd take the chance. Squatting on the ledge, he pulled off his boots, and, running a loop of pigging string through their loops, he slung them from his neck. Slipping thongs over his guns, he got into the chimney and braced his back against one side, then lifted his feet, first his left, then his right, against the opposite wall.

Whether Lisa was watching or not, he didn't know, but almost at that instant she began firing. The chimney was, at this point, all of six feet deep and wide enough to allow for climbing, but very risky climbing. His palms flat against the slippery wall, he began to inch himself upward, working his stocking feet up the opposite wall. Slowly, every movement a danger, his breath coming slowly, his eyes riveted on his feet, he began to work his way higher.

Sweat poured down his face and smarted in his eyes, and he could feel it trickling down his stomach under his wool shirt. Before he was halfway up, his breath was coming in great gasps, and his muscles were weary with the strain of opposing their strength against the walls to keep from falling. Then, miraculously, the chimney narrowed a little, and climbing was easier.

He glanced up. Not over twenty feet to go. His

heart bounded, and he renewed his effort. A foot slipped, and he felt an agonizing moment when fear throttled him and he seemed about to fall. To fall meant to bound from that ledge and go down, down into that deep green pool at the foot of the cliff, a fall of nearly 300 feet.

Something smacked against the wall near him and from below there was a shout. Then Lisa opened fire, desperately, he knew, to give him covering fire. Another shot splashed splinters in his face and he struggled wildly, sweat pouring from him, to get up those last few feet. Suddenly the rattle of fire ceased, and then opened up again. He risked a quick glance and saw Lisa Cochrane running out in the open, and, as she ran, she halted and fired.

She was risking her life, making her death or capture inevitable, to save him.

Suddenly a breath of air was against his cheek, and he hunched himself higher, his head reaching the top of the cliff. Another shot rang out and howled off the edge of the rock beside him. Then his hands were on the edge, and he rolled over onto solid ground, trembling in every limb.

There was no time to waste. He got to his feet, staggering, and stared around. He was on the very top of the mountain, and Tucker lay far away to the south. He seated himself and got his boots on, then slipped the thongs from his guns. Walking as swiftly as his still-trembling muscles would allow, he started south.

There was a creek, he remembered, that flowed down into the flatlands from somewhere near there, an intermittent stream, but with a cañon that offered an easy outlet to the plain below. Studying the terrain, he saw a break in the rocky plateau that might be it and started down the steep mountainside through the cedar, toward that break.

A horse was what he needed most. With a good horse under him, he might make it. He had a good lead, for they must come around the mountain, a good ten miles by the quickest trail. That ten miles might get him to town before they could catch him, to town and to the lawyer who would make the bid for them, even if Eaton had him in jail by that time. Suddenly, remembering how Lisa had run out into the open, risking her life to protect him, he realized he would willingly give his own to save her.

He stopped, mopping his face with a handkerchief. The cañon broke away before him, and he dropped into it, sliding and climbing to the bottom. When he reached the bottom, he started off toward the flat country at a swinging stride. A half hour later, his shirt dark with sweat, the cañon suddenly spread widely into the flat country. Dust hung in the air, and he slowed down, hearing voices.

"Give 'em a blow." It was a man's voice speaking. "Hear any more shootin'?"

"Not me." The second voice was thin and nasal. "Reckon it was my ears mistakin' themselves."

"Let's go, Eaton," another voice said. "It's too hot

45

here. I'm pinin' for some o' that good XY well water."

Gatlin pushed his way forward. "Hold it, Sheriff. You huntin' me?"

Sheriff Eaton was a tall, gray-haired man with a handlebar mustache and keen blue eyes. "If you're Gatlin, an' from the looks of you, you must be, I sure am. How come you're so all-fired anxious to get caught?"

Gatlin explained swiftly. "Lisa Cochrane's back there, an' they got her," he finished. "Sheriff, I'd be mighty pleased if you'd send a few men after her, or go yourself an' let the rest of them go to Tucker with me."

Eaton studied him. "What you want in Tucker?"

"To bid that ranch in for Lisa Cochrane," he said flatly. "Sheriff, that girl saved my bacon back there, an' I'm a grateful man. You get me to town to get that money in Lawyer Ashton's hands, an' I'll go to jail."

Eaton rolled his chaw in his lean jaws. "Dave Butler come over the Cut-Off with me, seen this ranch, then, an' would have it no other way but that he come back here to settle. I reckon I know what he wanted." He turned. "Doc, you'll git none of that XY water today. Take this man to Ashton, then put him in jail. An' make her fast."

Doc was a lean, saturnine man with a lantern jaw and cold eyes. He glanced at Gatlin, then nodded. "If you say so, Sheriff. I sure was hopin' for some o' that good XY water, though. Come on, pardner."

46

They wheeled their horses and started for Tucker, Doc turning from the trail to cross the desert through a thick tangle of cedar and sagebrush. "Mite quicker thisaway. Ain't nobody ever rides it, an' she's some rough."

It was high noon, and the sun was blazing. Doc led off, casting only an occasional glance back at Gatlin. Jim was puzzled, for the man made no show of guarding him. Was he deliberately offering him the chance to make a break? It looked it, but Jim wasn't having any. His one idea was to get to Tucker, see Ashton, and get his money down. They rode on, pushing through the dancing heat waves, no breeze stirring the air, and the sun turning the bowl into a baking oven.

Doc slowed the pace a little. "Hosses won't stand it," he commented, then glanced at Gatlin. "I reckon you're honest. You had a chance for a break an' didn't take it." He grinned wryly. "Not that you'd have got far. This here rifle o' mine sure shoots where I aim it at.

"I've nothin' to run from," Gatlin replied. "What I've said was true. My bein' in Tucker was strictly accidental."

The next half mile they rode side-by-side, entering now into a devil's playground of boulders and arroyos. Doc's hand went out, and Jim drew up. Buzzards roosted in a tree not far off the trail, a half dozen of the great birds. "Somethin' dead," Doc said. "Let's have a look."

200 yards farther and they drew up. What had been a dappled gray horse lay in a saucer-like depression among the cedars. Buzzards lifted from it, flapping their great wings. Doc's eyes glinted, and he spat. "Jim Walker's mare," he said, "an' his saddle."

They pushed on, circling the dead horse.

Gatlin pointed. "Look," he said, "he wasn't killed. He was crawlin' away."

"Yeah"—Doc was grim—"but not far. Look at the blood he was losin'."

They got down from their horses, their faces grim. Both men knew what they'd find, and neither man was looking forward to the moment. Doc slid his rifle from the scabbard. "Jim Walker was by way o' bein' a friend o' mine," he said. "I take his goin' right hard."

The trail was easy. Twice the wounded man had obviously lain still for a long time. They found torn cloth where he had ripped up his shirt to bandage a wound. They walked on until they saw the gray rocks and the foot of the low bluff. It was a *cul-de-sac*.

"Wait a minute," Gatlin said. "Look at this." He indicated the tracks of a man who had walked up the trail. He had stopped there, and there was blood on the sage, spattered blood. The faces of the men hardened, for the deeper impression of one foot, the way the step was taken, and the spattered blood told but one thing. The killer had walked up and kicked the wounded man.

They had little farther to go. The wounded man had

nerve, and nothing had stopped him. He was backed up under a clump of brush that grew from the side of the bluff, and he lay on his face. That was an indication to these men that Walker had been conscious for some time, that he had sought a place where the buzzards couldn't get at him.

Doc turned, and his gray white eyes were icy. "Step your boot beside that track," he said, his rifle partly lifted.

Jim Gatlin stared back at the man and felt cold and empty inside. At that moment, familiar with danger as he was, he was glad he wasn't the killer. He stepped over to the tracks and made a print beside them. His boot was almost an inch shorter and of a different type.

"Didn't figger so," Doc said. "But I aimed to make sure."

"On the wall there," Gatlin said. "He scratched somethin'."

Both men bent over. It was plain, scratched with an edge of whitish rock on the slate of a small slab— Cary done—and no more.

Doc straightened. "He can wait a few hours more. Let's get to town."

Tucker's street was more crowded than usual when they rode up to Ashton's office and swung down. Jim Gatlin pulled open the door and stepped in. The tall, gray-haired man behind the desk looked up.

"You're Ashton?" Gatlin demanded. At the

49

answering nod, he opened his shirt and unbuckled his money belt. "There's ten thousand there. Bid in the XY for Cochrane an' Gatlin."

Ashton's eyes sparkled with sudden satisfaction. "You're her partner?" he asked. "You're putting up the money? It's a fine thing you're doing, man."

"I'm a partner only in name. My gun backs the brand, that's all. She may need a gun behind her for a little while, an' I've got it."

He turned to Doc, but the man was gone. Briefly Gatlin explained what they had found and added: "Wing Cary's headed for town now."

"Headed for town?" Ashton's head jerked around. "He's here. Came in about twenty minutes ago."

Jim Gatlin spun on his heel and strode from the office. On the street, pulling his hat brim low against the glare, he stared left, then right. There were men on the street, but they were drifting inside now. There was no sign of the man called Doc or of Cary.

Gatlin's heels were sharp and hard on the board-walk. He moved swiftly, his hands swinging along-side his guns. His hard brown face was cool, and his lips were tight. At the Barrelhouse, he paused, put up his left hand, and stepped in. All faces turned toward him, but none was that of Cary.

"Seen Wing Cary?" he demanded. "He murdered Jim Walker."

Nobody replied, and then an oldish man turned his head and jerked it down the street. "He's gettin' his

50

hair cut, right next to the livery barn. Waitin' for the auction to start up."

Gatlin stepped back through the door. A dark figure, hunched near the blacksmith shop, jerked back from sight. Jim hesitated, alert to danger, then quickly pushed on.

The red and white barber pole marked the frame building. Jim opened the door and stepped in. A sleeping man snored with his mouth open, his back to the street wall. The bald barber looked up, swallowed, and stepped back.

Wing Cary sat in the chair, his hair half trimmed, the white cloth draped around him. The opening door and sudden silence made him look up. "You, is it?" he said.

"It's me. We found Jim Walker. He marked your name, Cary, as his killer."

Cary's lips tightened, and suddenly a gun bellowed, and something slammed Jim Gatlin in the shoulder and spun him like a top, smashing him sidewise into the door. That first shot saved him from the second. Wing Cary had held a gun in his lap and fired through the white cloth. There was sneering triumph in his eyes, and, as though time stood still, Jim Gatlin saw the smoldering of the black-rimmed circles of the holes in the cloth.

He never remembered firing, but suddenly Cary's body jerked sharply, and Jim felt the gun buck in his hand. He fired again then, and Wing's face twisted and his gun exploded into the floor, narrowly missing his own foot.

51

Wing started to get up, and Gatlin fired the third time, the shot nicking Wing's ear and smashing a shaving cup, spattering lather. The barber was on his knees in one corner, holding a chair in front of him. The sleeping man had dived through the window, glass and all.

Men came running, and Jim leaned back against the door. One of the men was Doc, and he saw Sheriff Eaton, and then Lisa tore them aside and ran to him. "Oh, you're hurt! You've been shot! You've . . . !"

His feet gave away slowly, and he slid down the door to the floor. Wing Cary still sat in the barbershop, his hair half clipped.

Doc stepped in and glanced at him, then at the barber. "You can't charge him for it, Tony. You never finished."

Grub Line Rider

I

There was good grass in these high meadows, Kim Sartain reflected, and it was a wonder they were not in use. Down below in the flatland the cattle looked scrawny and half starved. He had come up a narrow, little-used trail from the level country and was heading across the divide when he ran into the series of green, tree-bordered meadows scattered among the ridges.

Wind rippled the grass in long waves across the meadow, and the sun lay upon it like a caress. Across the meadow and among the trees he heard a vague sound of falling water, and turned the zebra dun toward it. As he did so, three horsemen rode out of the trees, drawing up sharply when they saw him.

He rode on, walking the dun, and the three wheeled their mounts and came toward him at a canter. A tall man rode a gray horse in the van. The other two were obviously cowhands, and all wore guns. The tall man had a lean, hard face with a knife scar across his cheek. "You there!" he roared, reining in. "What you doin' ridin' here?"

Kim Sartain drew up, his lithe, trail-hardened body easy in the saddle. "Why, I'm ridin' through," he said quietly, "and in no particular hurry. You got this country fenced against travel?"

53

"Well, it ain't no trail!" The big man's eyes were gray and hostile. "You just turn around and ride back the way you come! The trail goes around through Ryerson."

"That's twenty miles out of my way," Kim objected, "and this here's a nice ride. I reckon I'll keep on the way I'm goin'."

The man's eyes hardened. "Did Monaghan put you up to this?" he demanded. "Well, if he did, it's time he was taught a lesson. We'll send you back to him fixed up proper. Take him, boys!"

The men started, then froze. The six-shooter in Kim's hand wasn't a hallucination. "Come on," Kim invited mildly. "Take me."

The men swallowed and kept quietly in the saddle. The tall man's face grew red with fury. "So? A gunslinger, is it? Two can play at that game! I'll have Clay Tanner out here before the day is over!"

Kim Sartain felt his pulse jump. Clay Tanner? Why, the man was an outlaw, a vicious killer, wanted in a dozen places. "Listen, Big Eye," he said harshly, "I don't know you and I never heard of Monaghan, but if he dislikes you, that's one credit for him. Anybody who would hire or have anything to do with the likes of Clay Tanner is a coyote."

The man's face purpled and his eyes turned mean. "I'll tell Clay that!" he blustered. "He'll be mighty glad to hear it! That will be all he needs to come after you!"

Sartain calmly returned his gun to its holster,

keeping his eyes on the men before him without hiding his contempt. "If you *hombres* feel lucky," he said, "try and drag iron. I'd as soon blast you out of your saddles as not. As for you"—Kim's eyes turned on the tall man—"you'd best learn now as later how to treat strangers. This country ain't fenced and, from the look of it, ain't used. You've no right to keep anybody out of here, and, when I want to ride through, I'll ride through. Get me?"

One of the hands broke in, his voice edged: "Stranger, after talkin' that way to Jim Targ, you'd better light a shuck out of this country. He runs it."

Kim shoved his hat back on his head and looked from the cowhand to his boss. He was a quiet-mannered young drifter who liked few things better than a fight. Never deliberately picking trouble, he nevertheless had a reckless liking for it and never sidestepped any that came his way.

"He don't run me," he commented cheerfully, "and, personally, I think he's a mighty small pebble in a mighty big box. He rattles a lot, but for a man who runs this country, he fits mighty loose."

Taking out his tobacco, he calmly began to roll a smoke, his half smile daring the men to draw. "Just what," he asked, "gave you the idea you did run this country? And just who is this Monaghan?"

Targ's eyes narrowed. "You know damned well who he is!" he declared angrily. "He's nothin' but a two-by-twice would-be cattleman who's hornin' in on my range!"

"Such as this?" Kim waved a hand around him. "I'd say there ain't been a critter on this in months. What are you tryin' to do? Claim all the grass in the country?"

"It's my grass!" Targ declared belligerently. "Mine! Just because I ain't built a trail into it yet is no reason why. . . ."

"So that's it." Sartain studied them thoughtfully. "All right, Targ, you an' your boys turn around and head right out of here. I think I'll homestead this piece!"

"You'll what?" Targ bellowed. Then he cursed bitterly.

"Careful, Beetle Puss!" Kim warned, grinning. "Don't make me pull your ears!"

With another foul name, Targ's hand flashed for his gun, but no more had his fist grabbed the butt than he was looking again into the muzzle of Kim's six-shooter.

"I'm not anxious to kill you, Targ, so don't force it on me," he said quietly.

The cattleman's face was gray, realizing his narrow escape. Slowly, yet reluctantly, his hand left his gun.

"This ain't over!" Targ declared harshly. "You ride out of here, or we'll ride you out!"

As the three drifted away, Kim watched them go, then shrugged. "What the devil, pard," he said to the dun, "we weren't really goin' no place particular. Let's have a look around and then go see this Monaghan."

56

II

While the sun was hiding its face behind the western pines, Kim Sartain cantered the dun down into the cup-like valley that held the ranch buildings of the Y7. They were solidly built buildings, and everything looked sharp and clean. It was no rawhide outfit, this one of Tom Monaghan's. And there was nothing rawhide about the slim, attractive girl with red hair who came out of the ranch house and shaded her eyes at him.

He drew rein and shoved his hat back. "Ma'am," he said, "I rode in here huntin' Tom Monaghan, but I reckon I was huntin' the wrong person. You'd likely be the boss of any spread you're on. I always notice," he added, "that red-headed women are apt to be bossy."

"And I notice," she said sharply, "that drifting, no-good cowhands are apt to be smart. Too smart! Before you ask any questions, we don't need any hands. Not even top hands, if you call yourself that. If you're ridin' the grub line, just sit around until you hear grub call, then light in. We'd feed anybody, stray dogs or no-account saddle bums not barred. My name's Rusty."

Kim grinned at her. "All right, Rusty. I'll stick around for chuck. Meanwhile, we'd better round up Tom Monaghan, because I want to make him a little deal on some cattle."

"You? Buy cattle?" Her voice was scornful. "You're just a big-talking drifter." Her eyes flashed at him, but he noticed there was lively curiosity in her blue eyes.

"Goin' to need some cows," he said, curling a leg around the saddle horn. "Aim to homestead up there in the high meadows."

The girl had started to turn away, now she stopped and her eyes went wide. "You aim to *what?*"

Neither had noticed the man with iron-gray hair who had stopped at the corner of the house. His eyes were riveted on Sartain. "Yes," he said. "Repeat that again, will you? You plan to homestead up in the mountains?"

"Uhn-huh, I sure do." Kim Sartain looked over at Tom Monaghan and liked what he saw. "I've got just sixty dollars in money, a good horse, a rope, and a will. I aim to get three hundred head of cows from you and a couple of horses, two pack mules, and some grub."

Rusty opened her mouth to explode, but Tom held up his hand. "And just how, young man, do you propose to pay for all that with sixty dollars?"

Kim smiled. "Why, Mister Monaghan, I figure I can fatten my stock right fast on that upland grass, sell off enough to pay interest and a down payment on the principal. Next year I could do better. Of course," he added, "six hundred head of stock would let me make out faster, and that grass up there would handle them, plumb easy. Better, too, if I had somebody to cook for me, and mend my socks. How's about it, Rusty?"

"Why, you insufferable, egotistical upstart!"

"From what you say, I'd guess you've been up there in the meadows," Monaghan said thoughtfully, "but did you see anyone there?"

"Uhn-huh. Three *hombres* was waitin' around. One of them had a scar on his face. I think they called him Jim Targ."

Sartain was enjoying himself now. He had seen the girl's eyes widen at the mention of the men, and especially of Jim Targ. He kept his dark face inscrutable.

"They didn't say anything to you?" Monaghan was unbelieving. "Nothing at all?"

"Oh, yeah. This here Targ, he seemed right put out at my ridin' through the country. Ordered me to go around by Ryerson. Right about then I started lookin' that grass over, and sort of made up my mind to stay. He seemed to think you'd sent me up there."

"Did you tell him you planned to homestead?"

"Oh, sure. He didn't seem to cotton to the idea very much. Mentioned some *hombre* named Clay Tanner who would run me off."

"Tanner is a dangerous killer," Monaghan told him grimly.

"Oh, he is? Well, now. *Tsk, tsk, tsk.* This Targ's sort of cuttin' a wide swath, ain't he?"

The boarding-house triangle opened up suddenly with a deafening clangor, and Kim Sartain, suddenly aware that he had not eaten since breakfast, and little of that, slid off his horse. Without waiting for further comment, he led the dun toward the corral and began stripping the saddle.

"Dad"—Rusty moved toward her father—"is he crazy or are we? Do you suppose he really saw Targ?"

Tom Monaghan stared at Sartain thoughtfully, noting the two low-slung guns, the careless, easy swing of Kim's stride. "Rusty, I don't think he's crazy. I think maybe Targ is. I'm going to let him have the cows."

"Father!" She was aghast. "You wouldn't! Not three hundred!"

"Six hundred," he corrected. "Six hundred can be made to pay. And I think it will be worth it to see what happens. I've an idea more happened up there today than we have heard. I think that somebody tried to walk on this man's toes, and he probably happens to have corns on every one of them."

When their meal was finished, Monaghan looked over at Kim, who had had little to say during the supper. "How soon would you want that six hundred head?" He paused. "Next week?"

The four cowhands looked up, startled, but Kim failed to turn a hair. "Tomorrow at daylight," Kim said coolly. "I want the nearest cattle you have to the home ranch and the help of your boys. I'm goin' to push cattle on that grass before noon."

Tom Monaghan's eyes twinkled. "You're sudden, young fellow, plumb sudden. You know Targ's riders will be up there, don't you? He won't take this."

"Targ's riders," Sartain said quietly, "will get there about noon or after. I aim to be there first. Incidentally," he said, "I'll want some tools to throw together a cabin . . . a good strong one. I plan to build just west of the water."

He turned suddenly toward Rusty, who had also been very quiet. As if she knew he intended speaking to her, she looked up. Her boy's shirt was open at the neck, and he could see the swell of her bosom under the rough material.

"Thought about that cookin' job yet?" he asked. "I sure am fed up on my own cookin'. Why, I'd even marry a cook to get her up there."

A round-faced cowhand choked suddenly on a big mouthful of food and had to leave the table. The others were grinning at their plates. Rusty Monaghan's face went pale, then crimson. "Are you," she said coolly, "offering me a job, or proposing?"

"Let's make it a job first," Kim said gravely. "I ain't had none of your cookin' yet. If you pass the exams, then we can get down to more serious matters."

Rusty's face was white to the lips. "If you think I'd cook for or marry such a pig-headed windbag as you are, you're wrong. What makes you think I'd marry any broken-down, drifting saddle tramp that comes in here? Who do you think you are, anyway?"

Kim got up. "The name, ma'am, is Kim Sartain. As to who I am, I'm the *hombre* you're goin' to cook for. I'll be leavin' early tomorrow, but I'll drop back the next day, so you fix me an apple pie. I like lots of fruit, real thick pie, and plenty of juice."

Coolly he strolled outside and walked toward the corral, whistling. Tom Monaghan looked at his daughter, smiling, and the hands finished their supper quickly and hurried outside.

III

It was daybreak, with the air still crisp, when Rusty opened her eyes suddenly to hear the lowing of cattle, and the shrill Texas yells of the hands, driving cattle. Hurriedly she dressed and stopped on the porch to see the drive lining out for the mountains. Far ahead, her eyes could just pick out a lone horseman, headed toward Gunsight Pass and the mountain meadows.

Her father came in an hour later, his face serious. He glanced at her quickly. "That boy's got nerve," he said. "Furthermore, he's a hand."

"But Dad," she protested, "they'll kill him. He's just a boy, and that Tanner is vicious. I've heard about him."

Monaghan nodded. "I know, but Baldy tells me this Sartain was *segundo* for Ward McQueen of the Tumbling K when they had that run-in with rustlers a few months back. According to Baldy, Sartain is hell on wheels with a gun."

She was worried despite herself. "Dad, what do you think?"

He smiled. "Why, honey, if that man is all I think he is, Targ had better light a shuck for Texas, and, as for you, you'd better start bakin' that apple pie."

"Father!" Rusty protested. But her eyes widened a little, and she stepped farther onto the porch, staring after the distant rider.

Kim Sartain was a rider without illusions. Born and bred in the West, he knew to what extent such a man as Jim Targ could and would go. He knew that with tough, gun-handy riders, he would ordinarily be able to hold all the range he wanted, and that high meadow range was good enough to fight for.

Sartain knew he was asking for trouble, yet there was something in him that resented being pushed around. He had breathed the free air of a free country too long and had the average American's fierce resentment of tyranny. Targ's high-handed manner had got his back up, and his decision had not been a passing fancy. He knew just what he was doing, and no matter what the future held, he was determined to move in on this range and to hold it and fight for it if need be.

There was no time to waste. Targ might take him lightly, and think his declaration had been merely the loud talk of a disgruntled cowhand, but on the other side the rancher might take him seriously and come riding for trouble. The cattle could come in their own good time, but he intended to be on the ground, and quickly.

The dun was feeling good and Kim let him stretch out in a fast canter. It was no time at all until he was riding up to the pool by the waterfall. He gave a sigh of relief, for he was the first man on the ground.

He jumped down, took a hasty drink, and let the dun drink. Next he picked the bench for his cabin, and put down the axe he had brought with him. Baldy had told him there was a saddle trail that came up the opposite side of the mountain and skirted among the cliffs to end near this pool. Leaving the horse, Kim walked toward it.

Yet before he had gone more than three steps, he heard a quick step behind him. He started to turn, but a slashing blow with a six-gun barrel clipped him on the skull. He staggered and started to fall, glimpsed the hazy outlines of his attacker, and struck out. The blow landed solidly, and then something clipped him again, and he fell over into the grass. The earth crumbled beneath him, and he tumbled, over and over, hitting a thick clump of greasewood growing out of the cliff, then hanging up in some manzanita.

The sound of crashing in the brush below him was the first thing he remembered. He was aware that he must have had his eyes open and been half-conscious for some time. His head throbbed abominably, and, when he tried to move his leg, it seemed stiff and clumsy. He lay still, recalling what had happened.

He remembered the blows he had taken, and then falling. Below him he heard more thrashing in the brush. Then a voice called: "Must have crawled off, Tanner! He's not down here!"

Somebody swore, and aware of his predicament Kim held himself rigid, waiting for them to go away. Obviously he was suspended in the clump of manzanita somewhere on the side of the cliff. Above him, he heard the lowing of cattle. The herd had arrived then. What of the boys with it?

It was a long time before the searchers finally went away and he could move. When he could, he got a firm grip on the root of the manzanita and then turned himself easily. His leg was bloody, but seemed unbroken. It was tangled in the brush, however, and his pants were torn. Carefully he felt for his guns. One of them remained in its holster. The other was gone.

Working with infinite care and as quietly as possible, he lowered himself down the steep face of the rocky bluff, using brush and projections until finally he was standing upright on the ground below. A few minutes' search beneath where he had hung in the brush disclosed his other pistol, hanging in the top of a mountain mahogany.

Checking his guns, he limped slowly down into the brush. Here weakness suddenly overcame him, and he slumped to a sitting position. He had hurt his leg badly, and his head was swimming.

He squinted his eyes, squeezing them shut and

opening them, trying to clear his brain. The hammering in his skull continued, and he sat very still, his head bulging with pain, his eyes watching a tiny lizard darting among the stones. How long he sat there he did not know, but when he got started moving again, he noticed that the sun was well past the zenith.

Obviously he had been unconscious for some time in the brush, and had lost more time now. Limping, but moving carefully, he wormed his way along the gully into which he had fallen and slowly managed to mount the steep, tree-covered face of the bluff beyond where he had fallen.

Then, lowering himself to the ground, he rested for a few minutes, before dragging himself on. He needed water, and badly. Most of all, he had to know what had happened. Apparently Targ was still in command of the situation. The herd had come through, but Monaghan's riders must have been driven off. Undoubtedly Targ had the most men. Bitterly he thought of his boasts to Rusty and what they had amounted to. He had walked into a trap like any child.

It took him almost an hour of moving and resting to get near the falls. Watching his chance, he slid down to the water and got a drink, and then, crouching in the brush, he examined his leg. As he had suspected, no bones were broken, but the flesh was badly lacerated from falling into the branches, and he must have lost a good deal of blood. Carefully he bathed the wound in the cold water from the pool, then bound it up as well as he could by tearing his shirt and using his handkerchief.

When he had finished, he crawled into the brush and lay there like a wounded animal, his eyes closed, his body heavy with the pulsing of pain in his leg and the dull ache in his skull.

Somehow he slept, and, when he awakened, he smelled smoke. Lifting his head, he stared around into the darkness. Night had fallen, and there was a heavy bank of clouds overhead, but beyond the pool was the brightness of a fire. Squinting his eyes, he could see several moving figures, and no one sitting down. The pool at this point was no more than twenty feet across, and he could hear their voices clearly and distinctly.

"Might as well clean 'em up now, Targ," somebody was saying in a heavy voice. "He pushed these cattle in here, an' it looks like he was trying to make an issue of it. Let's go down there tonight."

"Not tonight, Tanner." Targ's voice was slower, lighter. "I want to be sure. When we hit them, we've got to wipe them out, leave nobody to make any complaint or push the case. It will be simple enough for us to tell our story and make it stick if they don't have anybody on their side."

"Who rightly owns this range?" Tanner asked.

Targ shrugged. "Anybody who can hold it. Monaghan wanted it, and I told everybody to lay off. Told them how much I wanted it and what would happen if they tried to move in. They said I'd no right to hold range I wasn't usin', an' I told them to start something, an' I'd show 'em my rights with a gun. I like this country, and I mean to hold it. I'll get the cattle later. If any of these piddlin' little ranchers wants trouble, I'll give it to 'em."

"Might as well keep these cows and get the rest of what that Irishman's got," Tanner said. "We've got the guns. If they are wiped out, we can always say they started it, and who's to say we're wrong?"

"Sure. My idea exactly," Targ agreed. "I want that Monaghan's ranch, anyway." He laughed. "And that ain't all he's got that I want."

"Why not tonight? He's only got four hands, and one of them is bad hurt or dead. At least one more is wounded a mite."

"Uhn-uh. I want that Sartain first. He's around somewhere, you can bet on that. He's hurt and hurt bad, but we didn't find him at the foot of that cliff, so he must have got away somehow. I want to pin his ears back, good!"

Kim eased himself deeper into the brush and tried to think his way out. His rifle was on his horse, and what had become of the dun he did not know. Obviously the Monaghan riders had returned to the Y7, but it was he who had led Tom Monaghan into this fight, and it was up to him to get him out. But how?

The zebra dun, he knew, was no easy horse for a stranger to lay hands on. The chances were that the horse was somewhere out on the meadow, and his rifle with him. Across near the fire there were at least six men, and no doubt another one or two would be watching the trail down to the Y7.

It began to look as if he had taken a bigger bite than he could handle. Maybe Rusty was right, after all, and he was just a loud-talking, drifting saddle bum who could get into trouble but not out of it. The thought stirred him to action. He eased back away from the edge of the pool, taking his time and moving soundlessly. Whatever was done must be done soon.

The situation was simple enough. Obviously Monaghan and some of the small flatland ranchers needed this upper range, but Targ, while not using it himself, was keeping them off. Now he obviously intended to do more. Kim Sartain had started something that seemed about to destroy the people he called his friends. And the girl, too.

He swallowed that one. Maybe he wasn't the type for double harness, but if he was, Rusty Monaghan was the girl. And why shouldn't he be? Ward McQueen had been the same sort of *hombre* as himself, and Ward was marrying his boss—as pretty a girl as ever owned a ranch.

While he had decided to homestead this place simply because of Targ's high-handed manner, he could see that it was an excellent piece of range. From talk at the Y7 he knew there were more of these mountain meadows, and some of the other ranchers from below could move their stock up. His sudden decision, while based on pure deviltry, was actually a splendid idea.

His cattle were on the range, even if they still wore Monaghan's brand. That was tantamount to possession if he could make it stick, and Kim Sartain was not a man given to backing down when his bluff was called. The camp across the pool was growing quiet, for one after another of the men was turning in. A heavy-bodied, bearded man sat near the fire, half dozing. He was the one man on guard.

Quietly Kim began to inch around the pool, and by the time an hour had passed and the riders were snoring loudly, he had completed the circuit to a point where he was almost within arm's length of the nearest sleeper. *En route* he had acquired something else—a long, forked stick.

With infinite care, he reached out and lifted the belt and holster of the nearest rider, then, using the stick, retrieved those of the man beyond. Working his way around the camp, he succeeded in getting all the guns but those of the watcher, and those of Tanner. These last he deliberately left behind. Twice, he had to lift guns from under the edges of blankets, but only once did a man stir and look around, but as all was quiet and he could see the guard by the fire, the man returned to his sleep.

Now Kim got to his feet. His bad leg was stiff, and he had to shift it with care, but he moved to a point opposite the guard. This would be the risky part, and the necessity for taking chances. His Colt level at the guard, he tossed a pebble against the man's chest. The fellow stirred, but did not look up. The next one caught him on the neck, and the guard looked up to see Kim Sartain, a finger across his lips for silence, the six-shooter to lend authority.

The guard gulped loudly, then his lips slackened and his eyes bulged. The heavy cheeks looked sick and flabby. With a motion of the gun, Kim indicated the man was to rise. Clumsily the fellow got to his feet and, at Sartain's gesture, approached him. Then Sartain turned the man around, and was about to tie his hands when the fellow's wits seemed to return. With more courage than wisdom, he suddenly bellowed: "Targ! Tanner! It's him!"

Kim Sartain's pistol barrel clipped him a ringing blow on the skull, and the big guard went down in a heap. Looking across his body, Kim Sartain stood with both hands filled with lead pushers. "You boys sit right still," he said, smiling. "I don't aim to kill anybody unless I have to. Now all of you but Tanner get up and move to the left."

He watched them with cat's eyes as they moved, alert for any wrong move. When they were lined up opposite him, all either barefooted or in sock feet, he motioned to Tanner. "You get up. Now belt on your guns, but careful. Real careful."

The gunman got shakily to his feet, his eyes murderous. He had been awakened from a sound sleep to look into Sartain's guns and see the hard blaze of the eyes beyond them. Nor did it pass unnoticed that all the guns had been taken but his, and his eyes narrowed, liking that implication not a bit.

"Targ," Kim said coldly, "you and your boys listen to me. I was ridin' through this country a perfect stranger until you tried to get mean. I don't like to have nobody ridin' me, see? So I went to see Monaghan, who I'd never heard about until you mentioned him. I made a deal for cows, and I'm in these meadows to stay. You bit off more than you could chew. Moreover, you brought this yellow-streaked, coyote-killin' Tanner in here to do your gun slinging for you, I hear he's right good at it. And I hear he was huntin' me. The rest of you boys are mostly cowhands. You know the right and wrong of this as well as I do. Well, right here and now we're goin' to settle my claim on this land. I left Tanner his guns after takin' all yours because I figured he really wanted me. Now he'll get his chance. Afterwards, if any of the rest of you want me, you can buy in, one at a time. When the shootin's over here tonight, the fight's over."

His eyes riveted on Targ. "You hear that, Jim Targ? Tanner gets his chance, then you do, if you want it. But you make no trouble for Tom Monaghan, and no trouble for me. You're just a little man in a big country. You can keep your spread and run it small, or you can leave the country."

As he finished speaking, he turned back to Tanner. "Now, you killer for pay, you've got your guns. I'm going to holster mine." His eyes swung to the

72

waiting cowhands. "You"—he indicated an oldish man with cold blue eyes and drooping gray mustaches—"give the word."

With a flick of his hand, his gun dropped into its holster, and his hands to their sides. Jim Targ's eyes narrowed, but his cowhands were all attention. Kim Sartain knew his Western men. Even outlaws like a man with nerve and would see him get a break.

"Now!" The gray-mustached man yelled. "Go for 'em!"

Tanner spread his hands wide. "No! No!" He screamed the words. "Don't shoot!"

He was unused to meeting men face to face with an even break. The very fact that Sartain had left his guns for him, a taunt and a dare as well as an indication of Sartain's confidence, had wrecked what nerve the killer had.

Now he stepped back, his face gray. With death imminent, all the courage went out of him. "I ain't got no grudge ag'in' you!" he protested. "It was that Targ! He set me on to you!"

The man who had given the signal exploded with anger. "Well, of all the yellow, two-bit, four-flushin' windbags!" His words failed him. "And you're supposed to be tough," he said contemptuously.

Targ stared at Tanner, then shifted his eyes to Sartain. "That was a good play," he said. "But I made no promises. Just because that coyote has yellow down his spine is no reason I forfeit this range."

"I said," Sartain commented calmly, "the fighting

73

ends here." Stooping, he picked up one of the gun belts and tossed it to Targ's feet. "There's your chance, if you want a quick slide into the grave."

Targ's face worked with fury. He had plenty of courage, but he was remembering that lightning draw of the day before, and knew he could never match it, not even approach it. "I'm no gunfighter!" he said furiously. "But I won't quit! This here range belongs to me!"

"My cattle are on it," Kim said coolly. "I hold it. You set foot on it even once in the next year, and I'll hunt you down wherever you are and shoot you like a dog."

Jim Targ was a study in anger and futility. His big hands opened and closed, and he muttered an oath. Whatever he was about to say was cut off short, for the gray-mustached hand yelled suddenly: "Look out!"

Kim wheeled, crouched, and drew as he turned. Tanner, his enemy's attention distracted, had taken the chance he was afraid to take with Sartain's eyes upon him. His gun was out and lifting, but Kim's speed was as the dart of a snake's head, a blur of motion, then a stab of red flame. Tanner's shot plowed dust at his feet. Then the killer wilted at the knees, turned halfway around, and fell into the dust beside the fire.

Sartain's gun swung back, but Targ had not moved, nor had the others. For an instant, the tableau held, and then Kim Sartain holstered his gun.

"Targ," he said, "you've made your play, and I've called you. Looks to me like you've drawn to a pair of deuces."

For just a minute the cattleman hesitated. He had his faults, but foolishness was not one of them. He knew when he was whipped. "I guess I have," he said ruefully. "Anyway, that trail would have been pure misery a-buildin'. Saves us a sight of work."

He turned away, and the hands bunched around him. All but the man with the gray mustache. His eyes twinkled.

"Looks like you'll be needin' some help, Sartain. Are you hirin'?"

"Sure." Sartain grinned suddenly. "First thing, catch my horse . . . I've got me a game leg . . . and then take charge until I get back here."

The boarding-house triangle at the Y7 was clanging loudly when the dun cantered into the yard.

Kim dismounted stiffly and limped up the steps.

Tom Monaghan came to his feet, his eyes widened. The hands stared. Kim noted with relief that all were there. One man had a bandage around his head; another had his arm in a sling, his left arm, so he could still eat.

"Sort of wound things up," Sartain explained. "There won't be any trouble with Targ in the high meadows. Figured to drop down and have some breakfast."

Kim avoided Rusty's eyes but ate in silence. He

75

was on his second cup of coffee when he felt her beside him. Then, clearing a space on the table, she put down a pie, its top golden brown and bulging with the promise of fruit underneath.

He looked up quickly.

"I knew you'd be back," she said simply.

Desert Death Song

I

When Jim Morton rode up to the fire, three unshaven men huddled there, warming themselves and drinking hot coffee. Morton recognized Chuck Benson from the Slash Five. The other men were strangers.

"Howdy, Chuck," Morton said. "He still in there?"

"Sure is," Benson told him. "An' it don't look like he's figurin' on comin' out."

"I don't reckon to blame him. Must be a hundred men scattered about."

"Nigher two hundred, but you know Nat Bodine. Shakin' him out of these hills is going to be tougher'n shaking a 'possum out of a tree."

The man with the black beard stubble looked up sourly. "He wouldn't last long if they'd let us go in after him. I'd sure roust him out of there fast enough."

Morton eyed the man with distaste. "You think so. That means you don't know Bodine. Goin' in after him is like sendin' a houn' dog down a hole after a badger. That man knows these hills, every crack an' crevice. He can hide places an Apache would pass up."

The black-bearded man stared sullenly. He had thick lips and small, heavy-lidded eyes. "Sounds like maybe you're a friend of his'n. Maybe when we

77

get him, you should hang alongside of him."

Somehow the long rifle over Morton's saddle bows shifted to stare warningly at the man, although Morton made no perceptible movement. "That ain't a handy way to talk, stranger," Morton said casually. "Ever'body in these hills knows Nat, an' most of us been right friendly with him one time or another. I ain't takin' up with him, but I reckon there's worse men in this posse than he is."

"Meanin'?" The big man's hand lay on his thigh.

"Meanin' anything you like." Morton was a Tennessee mountain man before he came West, and gun talk was not strange to him. "You call it your ownself." The long rifle was pointed between the big man's eyes, and Morton was building a cigarette with his hands only inches away from the trigger.

"Forget it!" Benson interrupted. "What you two got to fight about? Blackie, this here's Jim Morton. He's lion hunter for the Lazy S."

Blackie's mind underwent a rapid readjustment. This tall, lazy stranger wasn't the soft-headed drink of water he had thought him, for everybody knew about Morton. A dead shot with rifle and pistol, he was known to favor the former, even in fairly close combat. He had been known to go up trees after mountain lions, and once, when three hardcase rustlers had tried to steal his horses, the three had ended up in Boot Hill.

"How about it, Jim?" Chuck asked. "You know Nat. Where'd you think he'd be?"

Morton squinted and drew on his cigarette. "Ain't no figurin' him. I know him, an' I've hunted alongside of him. He's almighty knowin' when it comes to wild country. Moves like a cat an' got eyes like a turkey buzzard." He glanced at Chuck. "What's he done? I heard some talk down to the Slash Five, but nobody seemed to have it clear."

"Stage robbed yestiddy. Pete Daley of the Diamond D was ridin' it, an' he swore the robber was Nat. When they went to arrest him, Nat shot the sheriff."

"Kill him?"

"No. But he's bad off, an' like to die. Nat only fired once, an' the bullet took Larrabee too high."

"Don't sound reasonable," Morton said slowly. "Nat ain't one to miss somethin' he aims to kill. You say Pete Daley was there?"

"Yeah. He's the on'y one saw it."

"How about this robber? Was he masked?"

"Uhn-huh, an' packin' a Winchester Forty-Four an' two tied-down guns. Big black-haired man, the driver said. He didn't know Bodine, but Pete identified him."

Morton eyed Benson. "I shouldn't wonder," he said, and Chuck flushed.

Each knew what the other was thinking. Pete Daley had never liked Bodine. Nat married the girl Pete wanted, even though it was generally figured Pete never had a look-in with her, anyway, but Daley had worn his hatred like a badge ever since. Mary

79

Callahan had been a pretty girl, but a quiet one, and Daley had been sure he'd win her.

But Bodine had come down from the hills and changed all that. He was a tall man with broad shoulders, dark hair, and a quiet face. He was a good-looking man, even a handsome man, some said. Men liked him, and women, too, but the men liked him best because he left their women alone. That was more than could be said for Daley, who lacked Bodine's good looks but made up for it with money.

Bodine had bought a place near town and drilled a good well. He seemed to have money, and that puzzled people, so hints began to get around that he had been rustling as well as robbing stages. There were those, like Jim Morton, who believed most of the stories were started by Daley, but no matter where they originated, they got around.

Hanging Bodine for killing the sheriff—the fact that he was still alive was overlooked and considered merely a technical question, anyway—was the problem before the posse. It was a self-elected posse, inspired to some extent by Daley and given a semi-official status by the presence of Burt Stoval, Larrabee's jailer.

Yet, to hang a man, he must first be caught, and Bodine had lost himself in that broken, rugged country known as Powder Basin. It was a region of some ten square miles backed against an even rougher and uglier patch of waterless desert, but the basin was bad enough itself.

Fractured with gorges and humped with fir-clad hogbacks, it was a maze where the juniper region merged into the fir and spruce and where the cañons were liberally overgrown with manzanita. There were at least two cliff dwellings in the area and a ghost mining town of some dozen ramshackle structures, tumbled-in and wind-worried.

"All I can say," Morton conceded finally, "is that I don't envy those who corner him . . . when they do, and if they do."

Blackie wanted no issue with Morton, yet he was still sore. He looked up. "What do you mean, *if* we do? We'll get him!"

Morton took his cigarette from his lips. "Want a suggestion, friend? When he's cornered, don't you be the one to go in after him."

II

Four hours later, when the sun was moving toward noon, the net had been drawn tighter, and Nat Bodine lay on his stomach in the sparse grass on the crest of a hogback and studied the terrain below.

There were many hiding places, but the last thing he wanted was to be cornered and forced to fight it out. Until the last moment, he wanted freedom of movement.

Among the searchers were friends of his, men with whom he had ridden and hunted, men he admired and liked. Now they believed him wrong, they believed him a killer, and they were hunting him down.

They were searching the cañons with care, so he had chosen the last spot they would examine, a bald hill with only the foot-high grass for cover. His vantage point was excellent, and he had watched with appreciation the care with which they searched the cañon below him.

Bodine scooped another handful of dust and rubbed it along his rifle barrel. He knew how far a glint of sunlight from a Winchester can be seen, and men in that posse were Indian fighters and hunters.

No matter how he considered it, his chances were slim. He was a better woodsman than any of them, unless it was Jim Morton. Yet that was not enough. He was going to need food and water. Sooner or later, they would get the bright idea of watching the water holes, and after that. . . .

It was almost twenty-four hours since he had eaten, and he would soon have to refill his canteen.

Pete Daley was behind this, of course. Trust Pete not to tell the true story of what happened. Pete had accused him of the hold-up right to his face when they had met him on the street. The accusation had been sudden, and Nat's reply had been prompt. He'd called Daley a liar, and Daley moved a hand for his gun. The sheriff sprang to stop them and took Nat's bullet. The people who rushed to the scene saw only the sheriff on the ground, Daley with no gun drawn, and Nat gripping his six-shooter. Yet it was not that of which he thought now. He thought of Mary.

What would she be thinking now? They had been married so short a time and had been happy despite the fact that he was still learning how to live in civilization and with a woman. It was a mighty different thing, living with a girl like Mary.

Did she doubt him now? Would she, too, believe he had held up the stage, and then killed the sheriff? As he lay in the grass, he could find nothing on which to build hope.

Hemmed in on three sides, with the waterless mountains and desert behind him, the end seemed inevitable. Thoughtfully he shook his canteen. It was nearly empty. Only a little water sloshed weakly in the bottom. Yet he must last the afternoon through, and by night he could try the water hole at Mesquite Springs, no more than a half mile away.

The sun was hot, and he lay very still, knowing that only the faint breeze should stir the grass where he lay if he were not to be seen.

Below him, he heard men's voices and from time to time could distinguish a word or even sentence. They were cursing the heat, but their search was not relaxed. Twice men mounted the hill and passed near him. One man stopped for several minutes, not more than a dozen yards away, but Nat held himself still and waited. Finally the man moved on, mopping sweat from his face. When the sun was gone, he wormed his way off the crest and into the manzanita. It took him over an hour to get within striking distance of Mesquite Springs. He stopped just in time. His nostrils caught the faint fragrance of tobacco smoke.

Lying in the darkness, he listened, and after a moment heard a stone rattle, then the faint *chink* of metal on stone.

When he was far enough away, he got to his feet and worked his way through the night toward Stone Cup, a spring two miles beyond. He moved more warily now, knowing they were watching the water holes.

The stars were out, sharp and clear, when he snaked his way through the reeds toward the cup. Deliberately he chose the route where the overflow from Stone Cup kept the earth soggy and high grown with reeds and dank grass. There would be no chance of a watcher waiting there on the wet ground, nor would the wet grass rustle. He moved close, but there, too, men waited.

He lay still in the darkness, listening. Soon he picked out three men, two back in the shadows of the rock shelf, one over under the brush but not more than four feet from the small pool's edge.

There was no chance to get a canteen filled there, for the watchers were too wide-awake. Yet he might manage a drink.

He slid his knife from his pocket and opened it carefully. He cut several reeds, allowing no sound. When he had them cut, he joined them and reached them toward the water. Lying on his stomach within only a few feet of the pool and no farther from the nearest watcher, he sucked on the reeds until the water started flowing. He drank for a long time, then drank again, the trickle doing little, at first, to assuage his thirst. After a while, he felt better.

He started to withdraw the reeds, then grinned and let them lay. With care, he worked his way back from the cup and got to his feet. His shirt was muddy and wet, and with the wind against his body he felt almost cold. With the water holes watched, there would be no chance to fill his canteen, and the day would be blazing hot. There might be an unwatched hole, but the chance of that was slight, and, if he spent the night in fruitless search of water, he would exhaust his strength and lose the sleep he needed. Returning like a deer to a resting place near a ridge, he bedded down in a clump of manzanita. His rifle cradled in his arm, he was almost instantly asleep.

Dawn was breaking when he awakened, and his nostrils caught a whiff of wood smoke. His pursuers were at their breakfasts. By now they would have found his reeds, and he grinned at the thought of their anger at having had him so near without knowing. Morton, he reflected, would appreciate that. Yet they would all know he was short of water.

Worming his way through the brush, he found a trail that followed just below the crest and moved steadily along in the partial shade, angling toward a towering hogback.

Later, from well up on the hogback, he saw three horsemen walking their animals down the ridge where he had rested the previous day. Two more were working up a cañon, and, wherever he looked, they seemed to be closing in. He abandoned the canteen, for it banged against brush and could be heard too easily. He moved back, going from one cluster of boulders to another, then pausing short of the ridge itself.

The only route that lay open was behind him, into the desert, and that way they were sure he would not go. The hogback on which he lay was the highest ground in miles, and before him the jagged scars of three cañons running off the hogback stretched their ugly length into the rocky, brush-blanketed terrain. Up those three cañons, groups of searchers were working. Another group had cut down from the north and come between him and the desert ghost town.

The far-flung skirmishing line was well disposed, and Nat could find it in himself to admire their skill. These were his brand of men, and they understood their task. Knowing them as he did, he knew how relentless they could be. The country behind him was open. It would not be open long. They were sure he would fight it out rather than risk dying of thirst in the desert. They were wrong.

Nat Bodine learned that himself, suddenly. Had he been asked, he would have accepted their solution, yet now he saw that he could not give up.

The desert was the true Powder Basin. The Indians

had called it the Place of No Water, and he had explored deeply into it in past years and found nothing. While the distance across was less than twenty miles, a man must travel twice that or more, up and down and around, if he would cross it, and his sense of direction must be perfect. Yet, with water and time, a man might cross it.

But Nat Bodine had neither. Moreover, if he went into the desert, they would soon send word and have men waiting on the other side. He was fairly trapped, and yet he knew that he would die in that waste alone before he surrendered to be lynched. Nor could he hope to fight off this posse for long. Carefully he got to his feet and worked his way to the crest. Behind him lay the vast red maw of the desert. He nestled among the boulders and watched the men below. They were coming carefully, still several yards away. Cradling his Winchester against his cheek, he drew a bead on a rock ahead of the nearest man and fired.

Instantly the searchers vanished. Where a dozen men had been in sight, there was nobody now. He chuckled. *That made 'em eat dirt*, he thought. *Now they won't be so anxious.*

The crossing of the crest was dangerous, but he made it and hesitated there, surveying the scene before him. Far away to the horizon stretched the desert. Before him, the mountain broke sharply away in a series of sheer precipices and ragged chasms, and he scowled as he stared down at them, for it seemed no descent could be possible from there.

III

Chuck Benson and Jim Morton crouched in the lee of a stone wall and stared up at the ridge from which the shot had come. "He didn't shoot to kill," Morton said, "or he'd have had one of us. He's that good."

"What's on his mind?" Benson demanded. "He's stuck now. I know that ridge, an' the only way down is the way he went up."

"Let's move in," Blackie protested. "There's cover enough."

"You don't know Nat. He's never caught until you see him down. I know the man. He'll climb cliffs that would stop a hossfly."

Pete Daley and Burt Stoval moved up to join them, peering at the ridge before them through the concealing leaves. The ridge was a gigantic hogback almost 1,000 feet higher than the plateau on which they waited. On the far side, it fell away to the desert, dropping almost 2,000 feet in no more than 200 hundred yards, and most of the drop in broken cliffs.

Daley's eyes were hard with satisfaction. "We got him now!" he said triumphantly. "He'll never get off that ridge! We've only to wait a little, then move in on him. He's out of water, too."

Morton looked with distaste at Daley. "You seem powerful anxious to get him, Pete. Maybe the sheriff ain't dead yet. Maybe he won't die. Maybe his story of the shootin' will be different."

Daley turned on Morton, his dislike evident. "Your opinion's of no account, Morton. I was there, and I saw it. As for Larrabee, if he ain't dead, he soon will be. If you don't like this job, why don't you leave?"

Jim Morton stroked his chin calmly. "Because I aim to be here if you get Bodine," he said, "an' I personally figure to see he gets a fair shake. Furthermore, Daley, I'm not beholdin' to you, no way, an' I ain't scared of you. Howsoever, I figure you've got a long way to go before you get Bodine."

High on the ridge, flat on his stomach among the rocks, Bodine was not so sure. He mopped sweat from his brow and studied again the broken cliff beneath him. There seemed to be a vaguely possible route, but at the thought of it his mouth turned dry and his stomach empty.

A certain bulge in the rock looked as though it might afford handholds, although some of the rock was loose, and he couldn't see below the bulge where it might become smooth. Once over that projection, getting back would be difficult if not impossible. Nevertheless, he determined to try.

Using his belt for a rifle strap, he slung the Winchester over his back, then turned his face to the rock and slid feet first over the bulge, feeling with his toes for a hold. If he fell from here, he could not drop less than 200 feet, although close in there was a narrow ledge only sixty feet down.

Using simple pull holds and working down with

his feet, Bodine got well out over the bulge. Taking a good grip, he turned his head and searched the rock below him. On his left, the rock was cracked deeply, with the portion of the face to which he clung projecting several inches farther into space than the other side of the crack. Shifting his left foot carefully, he stepped into the crack, which afforded a good jam hold. Shifting his left hand, he took a pull grip, pulling away from himself with the left fingers until he could swing his body to the left and get a grip on the edge of the crack with his right fingers. Then, lying back, his feet braced against the projecting far edge of the crack and pulling toward himself with his hands, he worked his way down, step by step and grip by grip, for all of twenty feet. There the crack widened into a chimney, far too wide to be climbed with a lie back, its inner sides slick and smooth from the scouring action of wind and water.

Working his way into the chimney, he braced his feet against one wall and his back against the other, and by pushing against the two walls and shifting his feet carefully, he worked his way down until he was well past the sixty-foot ledge. The chimney ended in a small cavern-like hollow in the rock, and he sat there, catching his breath.

Nat ran his fingers through his hair and mopped sweat from his brow. Anyway—he grinned at the thought—they wouldn't follow him down here!

Carefully he studied the cliff below him, then to the right and left. To escape his present position, he must make a traverse of the rock face, working his way gradually down. For all of forty feet of climb, he would be exposed to a dangerous fall or to a shot from above if they had dared the ridge. Yet there were precarious handholds and some inch-wide ledges for his feet.

When he had his breath, he moved out, clinging to the rock face and carefully working across it and down. Sliding down a steep slab, he crawled out on a knife-edge ridge of rock and, straddling it, worked his way along until he could climb down a farther face, hand over hand. Landing on a wide ledge, he stood there, his chest heaving, staring back up at the ridge. No one was yet in sight, and there was a chance that he was making good his escape. At the same time, his mouth was dry, and the effort expended in descending had increased his thirst. Unslinging his rifle, he completed the descent without trouble, emerging at last upon the desert below.

Heat lifted against his face in a stifling wave. Loosening the buttons of his shirt, he pushed back his hat and stared up at the towering height of the mountain, and even as he looked up, he saw men appear on the ridge. Lifting his hat, he waved to them.

IV

Benson was the first man on that ridge, and involuntarily he drew back from the edge of the cliff, catching his breath at the awful depth below. Pete Daley, Burt Stoval, and Jim Morton moved up beside him, and then the others. It was Morton who spotted Bodine first.

"What did I tell you?" he snapped. "He's down there on the desert!"

Daley's face hardened. "Why, the dirty. . . ."

Benson stared. "You got to hand it to him," he said. "I'd sooner chance a shoot-out with all of us than try that alone."

A bearded man on their left spat and swore softly. "Well, boys, this does it. I'm quittin'. No man that game deserves to hang. I'd say, let him go."

Pete Daley turned angrily but changed his mind when he saw the big man and the way he wore his gun. Pete was no fool. Some men could be bullied, and it was a wise man who knew which and when. "I'm not quitting," he said flatly. "Let's get the boys, Chuck. We'll get our horses and be around there in a couple of hours. He won't get far on foot."

Nat Bodine turned and started off into the desert with a long swinging stride. His skin felt hot, and the air was close and stifling, yet his only chance was to get across this stretch and work into the hills at a point where they could not find him.

All this time, Mary was in the back of his mind, her presence always near, always alive. Where was she now? And what was she doing? Had she been told?

Nat Bodine had emerged upon the desert at the mouth of a boulder-strewn cañon slashed deeply into the rocky flank of the mountain itself. From the mouth of the cañon there extended a wide fan of rock, coarse gravel, sand, and silt flushed down from the mountain by torrential rains. On his right, the edge of the fan of sand was broken by the deep scar of another wash, cut at some later date when the water had found some crevice in the rock to give it an unexpected hold. It was toward this wash that Bodine walked.

Clambering down the slide, he walked along the bottom. Working his way among the boulders, he made his way toward the shimmering basin that marked the extreme low level of the desert. Here, dancing with heat waves and seeming from a distance to be a vast blue lake, was one of those dry lakes that collect the muddy run-off from the mountains. Yet, as he drew closer, he discovered he had been mistaken in his hope that it was a *playa* of the dry type. Wells sunk in the dry type of *playa* often produce fresh cool water, and occasionally at shallow depths. This, however, was a pasty, water-surfaced *salinas*, and water found there would be salty and worse than none at all. Moreover, there was danger that he might break through the crust beneath the dry, powdery dust and into the slime below.

The *playa* was such that it demanded a wide detour from his path, and the heat there was even more intense than on the mountain. Walking steadily, dust rising at each footfall, Bodine turned left along the desert, skirting the *playa*. Beyond it, he could see the edge of a rocky escarpment, and this rocky ledge stretched for miles toward the far mountain range bordering the desert.

Yet the escarpment must be attained as soon as possible, for knowing as he was in desert ways and lore, Nat understood in such terrain there was always a possibility of stumbling on one of those desert tanks, or *tinajas*, which contain the purest water any wanderer of the dry lands could hope to find. Yet he knew how difficult these were to find, for hollowed by some sudden cascade or scooped by wind, they are often filled to the brim with gravel or sand and must be scooped out to obtain the water in the bottom.

Nat Bodine paused, shading his eyes toward the end of the *playa*. It was not much farther. His mouth was powder dry now, and he could swallow only with an effort.

He was no longer perspiring. He walked as in a daze, concerned only with escaping the basin of the *playa*, and it was with relief that he stumbled over a stone and fell headlong. Clumsily he got to his feet, blinking away the dust and pushing on through the rocks. He crawled to the top of the escarpment through a deep crack in the rock, and then walked on over the dark surface.

It was some ancient flow of lava, crumbling to ruin now, with here and there a broken blister of it. In each of them, he searched for water, but they were dry. At this hour, he would see no coyote, but he watched for tracks, knowing the wary and wily desert wolves knew where water could be found.

The horizon seemed no nearer, nor had the peaks begun to show their lines of age or the shapes into which the wind had carved them. Yet the sun was lower now, its rays level and blasting as the searing flames of a furnace. Bodine plodded on, walking toward the night, hoping for it, praying for it. Once he paused abruptly at a thin whine of sound across the sun-blasted air.

Waiting, he listened, searching the air about him with eyes suddenly alert, but he did not hear the sound again for several minutes, and, when he did hear it, there was no mistaking it. His eyes caught the dark movement, striking straight away from him on a course diagonal with his own.

A bee!

Nat changed his course abruptly, choosing a landmark on a line with the course of the bee, and then followed on. Minutes later, he saw a second bee, and altered his course to conform with it. The direction was almost the same, and he knew that water could be found by watching converging lines of bees. He could afford to miss no chance, and he noted the bees were flying deeper into the desert, not away from it.

Darkness found him suddenly. At the moment, the

horizon range had grown darker, its crest tinted with old rose and gold, slashed with the deep fire of crimson, and then it was night, and a coyote was yapping myriad calls at the stars.

In the coolness, he might make many miles by pushing on, and he might also miss his only chance at water. He hesitated; then his weariness conformed with his judgment, and he slumped down against a boulder and dropped his chin on his chest. The coyote voiced a shrill complaint then, satisfied with the echo against the rocks, ceased his yapping and began to hunt. He scented the man smell and skirted wide around, going about his business.

V

There were six men in the little cavalcade at the base of the cliff, searching for tracks. The rider found them there. Jim Morton calmly sitting his horse and watching with interested eyes but lending no aid to the men who tracked his friend, and there were Pete Daley, Blackie, Chuck Benson, and Burt Stoval. Farther along were other groups of riders.

A man worked a hard-ridden horse toward them, and he was yelling before he arrived. He raced up and slid his horse to a stop, gasping: "Call it off! It wasn't him!"

"What?" Daley burst out. "What did you say?"

"I said . . . it wa'n't Bodine! We got our outlaw this mornin' out east of town! Mary Bodine spotted a man hidin' in the brush below Wenzel's place, an' she come down to town. It was him, all right. He had the loot on him, an' the stage driver identified him!"

Pete Daley stared, his little eyes tightening. "What about the sheriff?" he demanded.

"He's pullin' through." The rider stared at Daley. "He said it was his fault he got shot. His an' your'n. He said if you'd kept your fool mouth shut, nothin' would have happened, an' that he was another fool for not lettin' you get leaded down like you deserved!"

Daley's face flushed, and he looked around angrily like a man badly treated. "All right, Benson. We'll go home."

"Wait a minute." Jim Morton crossed his hands on the saddle horn. "What about Nat? He's out there in the desert, an' he thinks he's still a hunted man. He's got no water. Far's we know, he may be dead by now."

Daley's face was hard. "He'll make out. My time's too valuable to chase around in the desert after a no-account hunter."

"It wasn't too valuable when you had an excuse to kill him," Morton said flatly.

"I'll ride with you, Morton," Benson offered.

Daley turned on him, his face dark. "You do an' you'll hunt you a job!"

Benson spat. "I quit workin' for you ten minutes ago. I never did like coyotes."

He sat his horse, staring hard at Daley, waiting to

see if he would draw, but the rancher merely stared back until his eyes fell. He turned his horse.

"If I were you," Morton suggested, "I'd sell out an' get out. This country don't cotton to your type, Pete." Morton started his horse. "Who's comin'?"

"We all are." It was Blackie who spoke. "But we better fly some white. I don't want that salty Injun shootin' at me!"

It was near sundown of the second day of their search and the fourth since the hold-up, when they found him. Benson had a shirt tied to his rifle barrel, and they took turns carrying it.

They had given up hope the day before, knowing he was out of water and knowing the country he was in.

The cavalcade of riders was almost abreast of a shoulder of sandstone outcropping when a voice spoke out of the rocks. "You huntin' me?"

Jim Morton felt relief flood through him. "Huntin' you peaceful," he said. "They got their outlaw, an' Larrabee owes you no grudge."

His face burned red from the desert sun, his eyes squinting at them, Nat Bodine swung his long body down over the rocks. "Glad to hear that," he said. "I was some worried about Mary."

"She's all right." Morton stared at him. "What did you do for water?"

"Found some. Neatest *tinaja* in all this desert."

The men swung down, and Benson almost stepped on a small, red-spotted toad.

"Watch that, Chuck. That's the boy who saved my life."

"That toad?" Blackie was incredulous. "How d' you mean?"

"That kind of toad never gets far from water. You only find them near some permanent seepage or spring. I was all in, down on my hands and knees, when I heard him cheeping. It's a noise like a cricket, and I'd been hearing it some time before I remembered that a Yaqui had told me about these frogs. I hunted and found him, so I knew there had to be water close by. I'd followed the bees for a day and a half, always this way, and then I lost them. While I was studyin' the lay of the land, I saw another bee, an' then another. All headin' for this bunch of sand rock. But it was the toad that stopped me."

They had a horse for him, and he mounted up.

Blackie stared at him. "You better thank that Morton," he said dryly. "He was the only one was sure you were in the clear."

"No, there was another," Morton said. "Mary was sure. She said you were no outlaw and that you'd live. She said you'd live through anything." Morton bit off a chew, then glanced again at Nat. "They were wonderin' where you make your money, Nat."

"Me?" Bodine looked up, grinning. "Minin' turquoise. I found me a place where the Indians worked. I been cuttin' it out an' shippin' it East." He stooped and picked up the toad, and put him carefully in the saddlebag. "That toad," he said emphatically, "goes home to Mary an' me. Our place is green an' mighty pretty, an' right on the edge of the desert, but with plenty of water. This toad has got him a good home from here on, and I mean a good home."

One Last Gun Notch

I

Morgan Clyde studied his face in the mirror. It was an even-featured, pleasant face. Neither the nose nor jaw was too blunt or too long. Now, after his morning shave, his jaw was still faintly blue through the deep tan, and the bronze curls above his face made him look several years younger than his thirty-five.

Carefully he knotted the black string tie on the soft gray shirt, and then slipped on his coat. When he donned the black, flat-crowned hat, he was ready. His appearance was perfect, with just a shade of studied carelessness. For ten years now, Morgan Clyde's morning shave and dressing had been a ritual from which he never deviated.

He slid the two guns from their holsters and checked them carefully. First the right, then the left. On the butt of the right-hand gun there were nine filed notches. On the left, three. He glanced at them thoughtfully, remembering.

That first notch had been for Red Bridges. That was the year they had run his cattle off. Bridges had come out to the claim when Clyde was away, cut his fence down, run his cattle off, and shot his wife down in cold blood.

Thoughtfully Morgan Clyde looked back into the

mirror. He had changed. In his mind's eye he could see that tall, loose-limbed young man with the bronze hair and boyish face. He had been quiet, peace-loving, content with his wife, his homestead, and his few cattle. He had a gift for gun handling, but never thought of it. That is, not until that visit by Bridges.

Returning home with a haunch of antelope across his saddle, he had found his wife and the smoking ruins of his home. He did not have to be told. Bridges had warned him to move, or else. Within him something had burst, and for an instant his eyes were blind with blood. When the moment had passed, he had changed.

He had known, then, what to do. He should have gone to the governor with his story, or to the U.S. marshal. And he could have gone. But there was something red and ugly inside him that had not been there before. He had swung aboard a little paint pony and headed for Peavey's Mill.

The town's one street had been quiet, dusty. The townspeople knew what had happened, because it had been happening to all homesteaders. Never for a moment did they expect any reaction. Red Bridges was too well known. He had killed too many times.

Then Morgan Clyde rode down the street on his paint pony, saw Bridges, and slid to the ground. Somebody yelled, and Bridges turned. He looked at Morgan Clyde's young, awkward length and laughed. But his hand dropped swiftly for his gun.

But something happened. Morgan Clyde's gun swung up first, spouting fire, and his two shots centered over Bridges's heart. The big man's fingers loosened, and the gun slid into the dust. Little whorls rose slowly from where it landed. Then, his face puzzled, his left hand fumbling at his breast, Red Bridges wilted.

He could have stopped there. Now, Morgan Clyde knew that. He could have stopped there, and should have stopped. He could have ridden from town and been left alone. But he knew Bridges was a tool, and the man who used the tool was Erik Pendleton in the bank. Bridges had been a gunman; Pendleton was not.

The banker looked up from his desk and saw death. It was no mistake. Clyde had walked up the steps, around the teller's cage, and opened the door of Pendleton's office.

The banker opened his mouth to talk, and Morgan Clyde shot him. He had deserved it.

The posse lost him west of the Brazos, and he rode on west into a cattle war. He was wanted then and no longer cared. The banker hadn't rated a notch, but the three men he killed in the streets of Fort Sumner he counted, and the man he shot west of Gallup.

There had been trouble in St. George, and then in Virginia City. After that, he had a reputation.

Morgan Clyde turned and stared at the huge old grandfather's clock. It remained his only permanent possession. It had come over from Scotland years ago, and his family had carried it westward when they went to Ohio, and later to Illinois, and then to Texas. He had intended sending for it when the homestead was going right, and everything was settled. To Diana and himself it had been a symbol of home, of stability.

What could have started him remembering all that? The past, he had decided long ago, was best forgotten.

II

He rode the big black down the street toward Sherman's office. He knew what was coming. He had been taking money for a long time from men of Sherman's stripe. Men who needed what force could give them but had nothing of force in themselves.

Sherman had several gunmen on his payroll. He kept them hating one another and grew fat on their hatred. Tom Cool was there, and the Earle brothers. Tough and vicious, all of them.

Perhaps it was this case this morning that had started him thinking. Well, that damned fool nester should have known better than to settle on that Red Basin land. It was Sherman's best grazing land, even if he didn't own it. But a kid like that couldn't buck Sherman. The man was a fool to think he could.

The thought of that other young nester came into his mind. He dismissed it with an impatient jerk of his head.

The Earle brothers, Vic and Will, were sitting in the bar as he passed through. The two big men looked up, hate in their eyes.

Sherman was sitting behind the desk in his office and he looked up, smiling, when Morgan Clyde came in. "Sit down, Morg," he said cheerfully. He leaned back in his chair and put his fingertips together. "Well, this is it. When we get this Hallam taken care of, the rest of the nesters will see we mean business. We can have that range clean by spring, an' that means I'll be running the biggest herd west of the Staked Plains."

Tom Cool was sitting in a chair tilted against the wall. He had a thin, hatchet face and narrow eyes. He was rolling a smoke now, and he glanced up as his tongue touched the edge of the yellow paper.

"You got the stomach for it, Morg?" he asked dryly. "Or would you rather I handle this one? I hear you was a nester once yourself."

Morgan Clyde glanced around casually, one brow lifting. "You handle my work?" He looked his contempt. "Cool, you might handle this job. It's just a cold-blooded killing, and more in your line. I'm used to men with guns in their hands."

Cool's eyes narrowed dangerously. "Yeah?" His voice was a hoarse whisper. "I can fill mine fast enough, Clyde, any time you want to unlimber."

"I don't shoot sitting pigeons," Morgan said quietly.

"Why, you. . . ." Tom Cool's eyes flared with

hatred, and his hand dropped away from the cigarette in a streak for his gun.

Morgan Clyde filled his hand without more than a hint of movement. Before a shot could crash, Sherman's voice cut through the hot tension of the moment with an edge that turned both their heads toward the leader. There was a gun in his hand.

Queerly Morgan was shocked. He had never thought of Sherman as a fast man with a gun, and he knew that Cool felt the same. Sherman a gunman! It put a new complexion on a lot of things. Clyde glanced at Tom Cool and saw the man's hand coming away from his gun. There had been an instant when both of them could have died. If not by their own guns, by Sherman's. Neither had been watching him.

"You boys better settle down," Sherman said, leaning back in his swivel chair. "Any shooting that's done in my outfit will be done by me."

He looked up at Clyde, and there was something very much like triumph in his eyes. "You're getting slow, Morg," Sherman said. "I could have killed you before you got your gun out."

"Maybe."

Sherman shrugged. "You go see this Hallam, Clyde. I want him killed, see? An' the house burned. What happens to his wife is no business of yours. I got other plans." He grinned, revealing broken teeth. "Yeah, I got other plans for her."

Clyde spun on his heel and walked outside. He was just about to swing into the saddle when Tom Cool drifted up. Cool spoke lowly and out the corner of his mouth. "Did you see that, Morg? Did you see the way he got that gun into action? That gent's poison. Why's he been keepin' that from us? Somethin' around here smells to high heaven." He took his belt up a notch. "Morg, let's move in on him together. Let's take this over. There's goin' to be a fortune out there in that valley. You got a head on you. You take care of the business, an' I'll handle the rough stuff. Let's take Sherman out of there. He's framin' to queer both of us."

Morgan Clyde swung into the saddle. "No sale, Tom," he said quietly. "Riding our trail, we ride alone. Anyway, I'm not the type to sell out or double-deal. When I'm through with Sherman, I'll tell him so to his face."

"He'll kill you!"

Clyde smiled wearily. "Maybe."

He turned his horse and rode away. So Sherman was a gunman.

Tom Cool was right, there was something very wrong about that. The man hired his fighting done, rarely carried a weapon, and no one had ever suspected he might be fast. That was a powerful weapon in the hands of a double-crosser. A man who was lightning with a gun and unsuspected.

After all, where did he and Cool stand? Sherman owed him $10,000 for dirty work done, for cattle run off, for forcing men to leave, for a couple of shootings. Tom Cool was in the same position. Now, with

Hallam out of the way and the nesters gone, he would no longer need either Cool or himself.

Suddenly Morgan Clyde remembered Sherman's broken teeth, his sly smile, his insinuating manner when he spoke of Hallam's wife. Oddly, for the first time, he began to see himself in a clear light. A hired gun for a man with the instincts of a rat. It wasn't a nice thought. He shook himself angrily, forcing himself to concentrate on the business at hand.

Vic Hallam was young, and he was green. He was, they said, a fine shot with a rifle, and a fair man with a gun when he got it out, but by Western standards he was pitifully slow. He was about twenty-six, his wife a mere girl of nineteen, and pretty. Despite his youth, Hallam was outspoken. He had led the resistance against Sherman, and had sworn to stay in Red Basin as long as he wished. He had every legal right to the land, and Sherman had none.

But Morgan Clyde had long ago shelved any regard for the law. The man with the fastest gun was the law along the frontier, and so far he had been fastest. If Sherman wanted the Red Basin, he'd get it. If it was over Hallam's dead body, then that's how it would be.

He had never backed out on a job yet, and never would. Hallam would be taken care of.

III

Morgan rode at a rapid trot, knowing very well what he had to do. Hallam was a man of a fiery temper, and it would be easy to goad him into grabbing for a gun.

Clyde shook his head, striving to clear it of upsetting thoughts. With the $10,000 he had coming, he could go away. He could find a new country, buy a ranch, and live quietly somewhere beyond the reach of his reputation. Yet even as he told himself that, he knew it was not true. A few years ago he might have done just that, but now it was too late. Wherever he went, there would be smoking guns, split seconds of blasting fire, and the thunder of shooting. And wherever he went, he would be pointed out as a killer.

The heat waves danced along the valley floor, and he reined in his horse, moving at a walk. In his mind he seemed to be back again in the house he had built with Diana, and he remembered how they had talked of having the clock.

Then he was riding around the cluster of rocks and into the ranch yard at Red Basin. Sitting warily, with his hands loose and ready, he rode toward the house. A young woman came to the door and threw out some water. When she looked up, she saw him.

He was close enough then, and her face went deathly pale. Her eyes widened a little. Something inside of him shrank. He knew she recognized him.

"What . . . what do you want?" she asked.

He looked down at her wide eyes. She was pretty, he decided.

"I want to see Mister Hallam, ma'am."

She hesitated. "Won't you get down and sit on the porch? He's gone out now, but he'll be back soon. He . . . he saw some antelope over by the Rim Rocks."

Antelope. Morgan Clyde stiffened a little, then relaxed. He had hard work to make believe this was real. The girl—why, she was almost the size of Diana and almost, he admitted, as pretty. And the house— there was the wash bench, the homemade furniture, just like their own place. And now Hallam was after antelope.

It was all the same, even the rifle in the corner. . . . Something in him leaped. The rifle. A moment ago it had stood in the corner, and now it was gone. Instinctively he threw himself from his chair—a split second before the shot blasted past his head.

Cat-like, he came to his feet. He twisted the rifle from the girl's hands before she could shoot again. Coolly he ejected the shells from the rifle and dropped them on the table. He looked at the girl, smiling with an odd light of respect in his eyes. He noted there wasn't a sign of fright or tears in hers.

"Nice try," he said quietly.

"You came here to kill my husband," she said. It wasn't an accusation; it was a flat statement.

"Maybe." He shrugged. "Maybe so."

"Why do you want to kill him?" she demanded fiercely. "What did he ever do to you?"

Morgan Clyde looked at her thoughtfully. "Nothing, of course. But this land is needed by someone else. Perhaps you should move off."

"We like it here!" she retorted.

He looked around. "It's nice. I like it, too." He pointed to the corner across the room. "There should be a clock over there, a grandfather's clock."

She looked at him, surprised. "We . . . we're going to have one. Someday."

He got up and walked over to the newly made shelves and looked at the china. It had blue figures running around the edges, Dutch boys and girls and mills.

He turned toward the window. "I should think you'd have it open on such a nice morning," he said. "More air. And I like to see a curtain stir in a light wind. Don't you?"

"Yes, but the window sticks. Vic was going to fix it, but he's been so busy."

Morgan Clyde picked up the hammer and drew the strips of molding from around the window, then lifted it out. Resting one corner on the table, he slipped his knife from his pocket and carefully shaved the edges. He tried the window twice before it moved easily. Then he replaced it, and nailed the molding back in position. He tried it again, sliding up the window. A light breeze stirred the curtain, and the girl laughed. He turned, smiling gravely.

The sunlight fell across the rough-hewn floor, and, when he raised his eyes, he could see a man riding down the trail.

Morgan Clyde turned slowly, and looked at the girl. Her eyes widened.

"No!" she gasped. "Please! Not that!"

Morgan Clyde didn't look back. He walked out to the porch and swung into the saddle. He reined the black around and started toward the approaching homesteader.

Before Hallam could speak, Clyde said: "Bad way to carry your rifle. Never can tell when you might need it."

"Clyde!" Hallam exclaimed sharply. "What . . . ?"

"Good morning, Mister Hallam," Morgan Clyde said, smiling a little. "Nice place you've got here."

He touched his heels to the black and rode away at a canter. Behind him, the man stared, frowning. . . .

It wasn't until Clyde was riding down the street of the town that he thought of what was coming. *This is it*, he said to himself. He had known there would have to be an end to this sort of thing, and this was it.

The Earle brothers were still in the bar. They looked up at him as he passed, their eyes hard. He stepped to the door of the office and opened it. Sherman was seated at the desk, and Tom Cool was tilted back on his chair against the wall. Nothing, apparently, had changed except himself.

"I'm quitting, Sherman," he said quietly. "You owe me ten thousand dollars. I want it now."

Sherman's eyes narrowed. "Hallam? What about him?" he demanded.

Morgan Clyde smiled thinly with amusement in his eyes. "He's taken care of. Very nicely, I think."

"What's this nonsense about quitting?" Sherman demanded.

"That's it. I'm quitting."

"You don't quit until I'm ready," Sherman snapped harshly. "I want to know what happened out there."

Clyde stepped carelessly to one side so that he could face Tom Cool, too. "Nothing happened," he said quietly. "They have a nice place there. A nice couple. I envied them, so I decided to let them stay."

"You decided?"

He's faster than I am, Clyde's brain told him, even as he moved. *He'll shoot first, anyway, so. . . .*

Morgan Clyde's gun roared, and the shot caught Tom Cool in the chest, even as the gunman's weapon started to swing up to shoot him. Clyde felt a bullet fan past his own face, but he shot Cool again before he turned. Something struck him hard in the body, and then in one leg. He went down, then staggered up, and emptied his gun into Sherman.

Sherman's body sagged, and a slow trickle of blood came from the corner of his mouth.

Turning, Clyde got to the office door, walking very straight. His brain felt light, even a little giddy. He opened the door precisely and stepped out into the barroom. Across the room, the Earles, staring wide-eyed, jerked out their guns.

Through the door behind him they could see Sherman's body sagging in death. They moved as one man. Gritting his teeth, Morgan Clyde triggered his gun. He shot them both.

Morgan Clyde almost made it to his horse before he fell, sprawling his length in the dust. Vaguely he heard a roar of horse's hoofs, and then he felt himself turned over onto his back. Vic Hallam was staring at him.

Morgan Clyde's breath came hoarsely. He looked up, remembering. "My place," he muttered thickly through the blood that frothed his lips. "There's a clock. Put . . . put it . . . in the corner."

There was sympathy and a deep understanding in Hallam's face. "Sure, that'd be fine. When you get well, we'll move it over together . . . on condition that you'll go partners on the homestead. . . . But why didn't you wait, man? I'd have come with you."

"Partners," Morgan Clyde said, and it seemed good to be able to smile. "That'd be fine. Just fine."

Ride, You Tonto Raiders

I

The rain, which had been falling steadily for three days, had turned the trail into a sloppy river of mud. Peering through the slanting downpour, Mathurin Sabre cursed himself for the quixotic notion that impelled him to take this special trail to the home of the man that he had gunned down.

Nothing good could come of it, he reflected, yet the thought that the young widow and child might need the money he was carrying had started him upon the long ride from El Paso to the Mogollons. Certainly neither the bartender nor the hangers-on in the saloon could have been entrusted with that money, and nobody was taking that dangerous ride to the Tonto Basin for fun.

Matt Sabre was no trouble hunter. At various times, he had been many things, most of them associated with violence. By birth and inclination, he was a Western man, although much of his adult life had been lived far from his native country. He had been a buffalo hunter, a prospector, and for a short time a two-gun marshal of a tough cattle town. It was his stubborn refusal either to back up or back down that kept him in constant hot water.

Yet some of his trouble derived from something more than that. It stemmed from a dark and bitter drive toward violence—a drive that lay deeply within him. He was aware of this drive and held it in restraint, but at times it welled up, and he went smashing into trouble—a big, rugged, and dangerous man who fought like a Viking gone berserk, except that he fought coldly and shrewdly.

He was a tall man, heavier than he appeared, and his lean, dark face had a slightly patrician look with high cheek bones and green eyes. His eyes were usually quiet and reserved. He had a natural affinity for horses and weapons. He understood them, and they understood him. It had been love of a good horse that brought him to his first act of violence.

He had been buffalo hunting with his uncle and had interfered with another hunter who was beating his horse. At sixteen, a buffalo hunter was a man and expected to stand as one. Matt Sabre stood his ground and shot it out, killing his first man. Had it rested there, all would have been well, but two of the dead man's friends had come hunting Sabre. Failing to find him, they had beaten his ailing uncle and stolen the horses. Matt Sabre trailed them to Mobeetie and killed them both in the street, taking his horses home.

Then he left the country, to prospect in Mexico, fight a revolution in Central America, and join the Foreign Legion in Morocco, from which he deserted after two years. Returning to Texas, he drove a trail herd up to Dodge, then took a job as marshal of a town. Six months later, in El Paso, he had become engaged in an altercation with Billy Curtin, and Curtin had called him a liar and gone for his gun.

With that incredible speed that was so much a part of him, Matt drew his gun and fired. Curtin hit the floor. An hour later, he was summoned to the dying man's hotel room.

Billy Curtin, his dark, tumbled hair against a folded blanket, his face drawn and deathly white, was dying. They told him outside the door that Curtin might live an hour or even two. He could not live longer.

Tall, straight, and quiet, Sabre walked into the room and stood by the dying man's bed. Curtin held a packet wrapped in oilskin. "Five thousand dollars," he whispered. "Take it to my wife . . . to Jenny, on the Pivotrock, in the Mogollons. She's in . . . in . . . trouble."

It was a curious thing that this dying man should place a trust in the hands of the man who had killed him. Sabre stared down at him, frowning a little.

"Why me?" he asked. "You trust me with this? And why should I do it?"

"You . . . you're a gentleman. I trust you to help her. Will you? I . . . I was a hot-headed fool. Worried . . . impatient. It wasn't your fault."

The reckless light was gone from the blue eyes, and the light that remained was fading.

"I'll do it, Curtin. You've my word . . . you've got the word of Matt Sabre."

For an instant, then, the blue eyes blazed widely

117

and sharply with knowledge. "You're . . . Sabre?"

Matt nodded, but the light had faded, and Billy Curtin had bunched his herd.

It had been a rough and bitter trip, but there was little farther to go. West of El Paso there had been a brush with marauding Apaches. In Silver City, two strangely familiar riders had followed him into a saloon and started a brawl. Yet Matt was too wise in the ways of thieves to be caught by so obvious a trick, and he had slipped away in the darkness after shooting out the light.

The roan slipped now on the muddy trail, scrambled up, and moved on through the trees. Suddenly, in the rain-darkened dusk, there was one light, then another.

"Yellow Jacket," Matt said with a sigh of relief. "That means a good bed for us, boy. A good bed and a good feed."

Yellow Jacket was a jumping-off place. It was a stage station and a saloon, a livery stable and a ramshackle hotel. It was a cluster of adobe residences and some false-fronted stores. It bunched its buildings in a corner of Copper Creek.

It was Galusha Reed's town, and Reed owned the Yellow Jacket Saloon and the Rincon Mine. Sid Trumbull was town marshal, and he ran the place for Reed. Wherever Reed rode, Tony Sikes was close by, and there were some who said that Reed in turn was owned by Prince McCarran, who owned the big PM brand in the Tonto Basin country.

Matt Sabre stabled his horse and turned to the slope-shouldered liveryman. "Give him a bait of corn. Another in the morning."

"Corn?" Simpson shook his head. "We've no corn."

"You have corn for the freighters' stock and corn for the stage horses. Give my horse corn."

Sabre had a sharp ring of authority in his voice, and, before he realized it, Simpson was giving the big roan his corn. He thought about it and stared after Sabre. The tall rider was walking away, a light, long step, easy and free, on the balls of his feet. And he carried two guns, low-hung and tied-down.

Simpson stared, then shrugged. "A bad one," he muttered. "Wish he'd kill Sid Trumbull."

Matt Sabre pushed into the door of the Yellow Jacket and dropped his saddlebags to the floor. Then he strode to the bar. "What have you got, man? Anything but rye?"

"What's the matter? Ain't rye good enough for you?" The bartender, a man named Hobbs, was sore himself. No man should work so many hours on feet like his.

"Have you brandy? Or some Irish whiskey?"

Hobbs stared. "Mister, where do you think you are? New York?"

"That's all right, Hobbs. I like a man who knows what he likes. Give him some of my cognac."

Matt Sabre turned and glanced at the speaker. He was a tall man, immaculate in black broadcloth, with

119

blond hair slightly wavy and a rosy complexion. He might have been thirty or older. He wore a pistol on his left side, high up.

"Thanks," Sabre said briefly. "There's nothing better than cognac on a wet night."

"My name is McCarran. I run the PM outfit, east of here. Northeast, to be exact."

Sabre nodded. "My name is Sabre. I run no outfit, but I'm looking for one. Where's the Pivotrock?"

He was a good poker player, men said. His eyes were fast from using guns, and so he saw the sudden glint and the quick caution in Prince McCarran's eyes.

"The Pivotrock? Why, that's a stream over in the Mogollons. There's an outfit over there, all right. A one-horse affair. Why do you ask?"

Sabre cut him off short. "Business with them."

"I see. Well, you'll find it a lonely ride. There's trouble up that way now, some sort of a cattle war."

Matt Sabre tasted his drink. It was good cognac. In fact, it was the best, and he had found none west of New Orleans.

McCarran, his name was. He knew something, too. Curtin had asked him to help his widow. Was the Pivotrock outfit in the war? He decided against asking McCarran, and they talked quietly of the rain and of cattle, then of cognac. "You never acquired a taste for cognac in the West. May I ask where?"

"Paris," Sabre replied, "Marseilles, Fez, and Marrakesh."

"You've been around, then. Well, that's not

uncommon." The blond man pointed toward a heavy-shouldered young man who slept with his head on his arms. "See that chap? Calls himself Camp Gordon. He's a Cambridge man, quotes the classics when he's drunk . . . which is over half the time . . . and is one of the best cowhands in the country when he's sober. Keys over there, playing the piano, studied in Weimar. He knew Strauss, in Vienna, before he wrote 'The Blue Danube'. There's all sorts of men in the West, from belted earls and remittance men to vagabond scum from all corners of the world. They are here a few weeks, and they talk the lingo like veterans. Some of the biggest ranches in the West are owned by Englishmen."

Prince McCarran talked to him a few minutes longer, but he learned nothing. Sabre was not evasive, but somehow he gave out no information about himself or his mission. McCarran walked away very thoughtfully. Later, after Matt Sabre was gone, Sid Trumbull came in.

"Sabre?" Trumbull shook his head. "Never heard of him. Keys might know. He knows about ever'-body. What's he want on the Pivotrock?"

Lying on his back in bed, Matt Sabre stared up into the darkness and listened to the rain on the window and on the roof. It rattled hard, skeleton fingers against the glass, and he turned restlessly in his bed, frowning as he recalled that quick, guarded expression in the eyes of Prince McCarran.

Who was McCarran, and what did he know? Had Curtin's request that he help his wife been merely the natural request of a dying man, or had he felt that there was a definite need of help? Was something wrong here?

He went to sleep vowing to deliver the money and ride away. Yet even as his eyes closed the last time, he knew he would not do it if there was trouble.

It was still raining, but no longer pouring, when he awakened. He dressed swiftly and checked his guns, his mind taking up his problems where they had been left the previous night.

Camp Gordon, his face puffy from too much drinking and too sound a sleep, staggered down the stairs after him. He grinned woefully at Sabre. "I guess I really hung one on last night," he said. "What I need is to get out of town."

They ate breakfast together, and Gordon's eyes sharpened suddenly at Matt's query of directions to the Pivotrock. "You'll not want to go there, man. Since Curtin ran out, they've got their backs to the wall. They are through! Leave it to Galusha Reed for that."

"What's the trouble?"

"Reed claims title to the Pivotrock. Bill Curtin's old man bought it from a Mex who had it from a land grant. Then he made a deal with the Apaches, which seemed to cinch his title. Trouble was, Galusha Reed shows up with a prior claim. He says Fernandez had no grant. That his man Sonoma had a prior one. Old

122

Man Curtin was killed when he fell from his buckboard, and young Billy couldn't stand the gaff. He blew town after Tony Sikes buffaloed him."

"What about his wife?"

Gordon shook his head, then shrugged. Doubt and worry struggled on his face. "She's a fine girl, Jenny Curtin is. The salt of the earth. It's too bad Curtin hadn't a tenth of her nerve. She'll stick, and she swears she'll fight."

"Has she any men?"

"Two. An old man who was with her father-in-law and a half-breed Apache they call Rado. It used to be Silverado."

Thinking it over, Sabre decided there was much left to be explained. Where had the $5,000 come from? Had Billy really run out, or had he gone away to get money to put up a battle? And how did he get it?

"I'm going out." Sabre got to his feet. "I'll have a talk with her."

"Don't take a job there. She hasn't a chance," Gordon said grimly. "You'd do well to stay away."

"I like fights when one side doesn't have a chance," Matt replied lightly. "Maybe I will ask for a job. A man's got to die sometime, and what better time than fighting when the odds are against him?"

"I like to win," Gordon said flatly. "I like at least a chance."

Matt Sabre leaned over the table, aware that Prince McCarran had moved up behind Gordon, and that a big man with a star was standing near him. "If I decide to go to work for her"—Sabre's voice was easy, confident—"then you'd better join us. Our side will win."

"Look here, you!" The man wearing the star, Sid Trumbull, stepped forward. "You either stay in town or get down the trail! There's trouble enough in the Mogollons. Stay out of there."

Matt looked up. "You're telling me?" His voice cracked like a whip. "You're town marshal, Trumbull, not a United States marshal or a sheriff, and, if you were a sheriff, it wouldn't matter. It is out of this county. Now suppose you back up and don't step into conversations unless you're invited."

Trumbull's head lowered, and his face flushed red. Then he stepped around the table, his eyes narrow and mean. "Listen, you!" His voice was thick with fury. "No two-by-twice cowpoke tells me . . . !"

"Trumbull"—Sabre spoke evenly—"you're asking for it. You aren't acting in line of duty now. You're picking trouble, and the fact that you're marshal won't protect you."

"Protect me?" His fury exploded. "Protect me? Why, you . . . !"

Trumbull lunged around the table, but Matt side-stepped swiftly and kicked a chair into the marshal's path. Enraged, Sid Trumbull had no chance to avoid it and fell headlong, bloodying his palms on the slivery floor.

Kicking the chair away, he lunged to his feet, and

Matt stood facing him, smiling. Camp Gordon was grinning, and Hobbs was leaning his forearms on the bar, watching with relish.

Trumbull stared at his torn palms, then lifted his eyes to Sabre's. Then he started forward, and suddenly, in mid-stride, his hand swept for his gun.

Sabre palmed his Colt, and the gun barked even as it lifted. Stunned, Sid Trumbull stared at his numbed hand. His gun had been knocked spinning, and the .44 slug, hitting the trigger guard, had gone by to rip off the end of Sid's little finger. Dumbly he stared at the slow drip of blood.

Prince McCarran and Gordon were only two of those who stared, not at the marshal, but at Matt Sabre.

"You throw that gun mighty fast, stranger," McCarran said. "Who are you, anyway? There aren't a half dozen men in the country who can throw a gun that fast. I know most of them by sight."

Sabre's eyes glinted coldly. "No? Well, you know another one now. Call it seven men." He spun on his heel and strode from the room. All eyes followed him.

II

Matt Sabre's roan headed up Shirt Tail Creek, crossed Bloody Basin and Skeleton Ridge, and made the Verde in the vicinity of the hot springs. He bedded down that night in a corner of a cliff near

Hardscrabble Creek. It was late when he turned in, and he had lit no fire.

He had chosen his position well, for behind him the cliff towered, and on his left there was a steep hillside that sloped away toward Hardscrabble Creek. He was almost at the foot of Hardscrabble Mesa, with the rising ground of Deadman Mesa before him. The ground in front sloped away to the creek, and there was plenty of dry wood. The overhang of the cliff protected it from the rain.

Matt Sabre came suddenly awake. For an instant, he lay very still. The sky had cleared, and, as he lay on his side, he could see the stars. He judged that it was past midnight. Why he had awakened he could not guess, but he saw that the roan was nearer, and the big gelding had his head up and ears pricked.

"Careful, boy," Sabre warned.

Sliding out of his bedroll, he drew on his boots and got to his feet. Feeling out in the darkness, he drew his Winchester near.

He was sitting in absolute blackness due to the cliff's overhang. He knew the boulders and the clumps of cedar were added concealment. The roan would be lost against the blackness of the cliff, but from where he sat, he could see some thirty yards of the creekbank and some open ground.

There was subdued movement below and whispering voices. Then silence. Leaving his rifle, Sabre belted on his guns and slid quietly out of the overhang and into the cedars.

After a moment, he heard the sound of movement, and then a low voice: "He can't be far. They said he came this way, and he left the main trail after Fossil Creek."

There were two of them. He waited, standing there among the cedars, his eyes hard and his muscles poised and ready. They were fools. Did they think he was that easy?

He had fought Apaches and Kiowas, and he had fought the Tauregs in the Sahara and the Riffs in the Atlas Mountains. He saw them then, saw their dark figures moving up the hill, outlined against the pale gravel of the slope.

That hard, bitter thing inside him broke loose, and he could not stand still. He could not wait. They would find the roan, and then they would not leave until they had him. It was now or never. He stepped out quickly, silently.

"Looking for somebody?"

They wheeled, and he saw the starlight on a pistol barrel and heard the flat, husky cough of his own gun. One went down, gasping. The other staggered, then turned and started off in a stumbling run, moaning half in fright, half in pain. He stood there, trying to follow the man, but he lost him in the brush.

He turned back to the fellow on the ground but did not go near him. He circled widely instead, returning to his horse. He quieted his roan, then lay down. In a few minutes, he was dozing.

Daybreak found him standing over the body. The roan was already saddled for the trail. It was one of the two he had seen in Silver City, a lean, dark-faced man with deep lines in his cheeks and a few gray hairs at the temples. There was an old scar, deep and red, over his eye.

Sabre knelt and went through his pockets, taking a few letters and some papers. He stuffed them into his own pockets, then mounted. Riding warily, he started up the creek. He rode with his Winchester across his saddle, ready for whatever came. Nothing did.

The morning drew on, the air warm and still after the rain. A fly *buzzed* around his ears, and he whipped it away with his hat. The roan had a long-striding, space-eating walk. It moved out swiftly and surely toward the far purple ranges, dipping down through grassy meadows lined with pines and aspens, with here and there the whispering leaves of a tall cottonwood.

It was a land to dream about, a land perfect for the grazing of either cattle or sheep, a land for a man to live in. Ahead and on his left he could see the towering Mogollon Rim, and it was beyond this rim, up on the plateau, that he would find the Pivotrock. He skirted a grove of rustling aspen and looked down a long valley.

For the first time, he saw cattle—fat, contented cattle, fat from the rich grass of these bottom lands. Once, far off, he glimpsed a rider, but he made no effort to draw near, wanting only to find the trail to the Pivotrock.

A wide-mouthed cañon opened from the northeast, and he turned the roan and started up the creek that ran down it. Now he was climbing, and from the look of the country, he would climb nearly 3,000 feet to reach the rim. Yet he had been told there was a trail ahead, and he pushed on.

The final 800 feet to the rim was by a switchback trail that had him climbing steadily, yet the air on the plateau atop the rim was amazingly fresh and clear. He pushed on, seeing a few scattered cattle, and then he saw a crude wooden sign by the narrow trail. It read: PIVOTROCK 1 MILE

The house was low and sprawling, lying on a flat-topped knoll with the long barns and sheds built on three sides of a square. The open side faced the rim and the trail up which he was riding. There were cottonwood, pine, and fir backing up the buildings. He could see the late afternoon sunlight glistening on the coats of the saddle stock in the corral.

An old man stepped from the stable with a carbine in his hands. "All right, stranger. You stop where you are. What you want here?"

Matt Sabre grinned. Lifting his hand carefully, he pushed back his flat-brimmed hat. "Huntin' Missus Jenny Curtin," he said. "I've got news." He hesitated. "Of her husband."

The carbine muzzle lowered. "Of him? What news would there be of him?"

"Not good news," Sabre told him. "He's dead."

Surprisingly the old man seemed relieved. "Light," he said briefly. "I reckon we figured he was dead. How'd it happen?"

Sabre hesitated. "He picked a fight in a saloon in El Paso, then drew too slow."

"He was never fast." The old man studied him. "My name's Tom Judson. Now, you sure didn't come all the way here from El Paso to tell us Billy was dead. What did you come for?"

"I'll tell Missus Curtin that. However, they tell me down the road you've been with her a long time, so you might as well know. I brought her some money. Bill Curtin gave it to me on his deathbed, asked me to bring it to her. It's five thousand dollars."

"Five thousand?" Judson stared. "Reckon Bill must have set some store by you to trust you with it. Know him long?"

Sabre shook his head. "Only a few minutes. A dying man hasn't much choice."

A door slammed up at the house, and they both turned. A slender girl was walking toward them, and the sunlight caught the red in her hair. She wore a simple cotton dress, but her figure was trim and neat. Ahead of her dashed a boy who might have been five or six. He lunged at Sabre, then slid to a stop, and stared up at him, then at his guns.

"Howdy, old-timer!" Sabre said, smiling. "Where's your spurs?"

The boy was startled and shy. He drew back, surprised at the question. "I . . . I've got no spurs!"

130

"What? A cowhand without spurs? We'll have to fix that." He looked up. "How are you, Missus Curtin? I'm Mathurin Sabre, Matt for short. I'm afraid I've some bad news for you."

Her face paled a little, but her chin lifted. "Will you come to the house, Mister . . . Sabre? Tom, put his horse in the corral, will you?"

The living room of the ranch house was spacious and cool. There were Navajo rugs upon the floor, and the chairs and the divan were beautifully tanned cowhide. He glanced around appreciatively, enjoying the coolness after his hot ride in the Arizona sun, like the naturalness of this girl, standing in the home she had created.

She faced him abruptly. "Perhaps you'd better tell me now. There's no use pretending or putting a bold face on it when I have to be told."

As quickly and quietly as possible, he explained. When he was finished, her face was white and still. "I . . . I was afraid of this. When he rode away, I knew he would never come back. You see, he thought . . . he believed he had failed me, failed his father."

Matt drew the oilskin packet from his pocket. "He sent you this. He said it was five thousand dollars. He said to give it to you."

She took it, staring at the package, and tears welled into her eyes. "Yes." Her voice was so low that Matt scarcely heard it. "He would do this. He probably felt it was all he could do for me, for us. You see"—

Jenny Curtin's eyes lifted—"we're in a fight, and a bad one. This is war money. I . . . guess Billy thought . . . well, he was no fighter himself, and this might help, might compensate. You're probably wondering about all this."

"No," he said. "I'm not. And maybe I'd better go out with the boys now. You'll want to be alone."

"Wait!" Her fingers caught his sleeve. "I want you to know, since you were with him when he died, and you have come all this way to help us. There was no trouble with Billy and me. It was . . . well, he thought he was a coward. He thought he had failed me. We've had trouble with Galusha Reed in Yellow Jacket. Tony Sikes picked a fight with Billy. He wanted to kill him, and Billy wouldn't fight. He . . . he backed down. Everybody said he was a coward, and he ran. He went . . . away."

Matt Sabre frowned thoughtfully, staring at the floor. The boy who picked a fight with him, who dared him, who went for his gun, was no coward. Trying to prove something to himself? Maybe. But no coward.

"Ma'am," he said abruptly, "you're his widow. The mother of his child. There's something you should know. Whatever else he was, I don't know. I never knew him long enough. But that man was no coward. Not even a little bit. You see . . . ,"—Matt hesitated, feeling the falseness of his position, not wanting to tell this girl that he had killed her husband, yet not wanting her to think him a coward—"I saw his eyes when he went for his gun. I was there, ma'am, and saw it all. Bill Curtin was no coward."

Hours later, lying in his bunk, he thought of it, and the $5,000 was still a mystery. Where had it come from? How had Curtin come by it?

He turned over and after a few minutes went to sleep. The next day, he would be riding.

The sunlight was bright the next morning when he finally rolled out of bed. He bathed and shaved, taking his time, enjoying the sun on his back, and feeling glad he was footloose again. He was in the bunkhouse, belting on his guns, when he heard the horses. He stepped to the door and glanced out.

Neither the dark-faced Rado nor Judson was about, and there were three riders in the yard. One of them he recognized as a man from Yellow Jacket, and the tallest of the riders was Galusha Reed. He was a big man, broad and thick in the body without being fat. His jaw was brutal.

Jenny Curtin came out on the steps.

"Ma'am," Reed said abruptly, "we're movin' you off this land. We're goin' to give you ten minutes to pack, an' one of my boys'll hitch the buckboard for you. This here trouble's gone on long enough, an' mine's the prior claim to this land. You're gettin' off."

Jenny's eyes turned quickly toward the stable, but Reed shook his head. "You needn't look for Judson or the 'breed. We watched until we seen them away from here, an' some of my boys are coverin' the trail. We're tryin' to get you off here without any trouble."

"You can turn around and leave, Mister Reed. I'm not going!"

"I reckon you are," Reed said patiently. "We know that your man's dead. We just can't put up with you squattin' on our range."

"This happens to be my range, and I'm staying."

Reed chuckled. "Don't make us put you off, ma'am. Don't make us get rough. Up here"—he waved a casual hand—"we can do anything we want, and nobody the wiser. You're leavin', as of now."

Matt Sabre stepped out of the bunkhouse and took three quick steps toward the riders. He was cool and sure of himself, but he could feel the jumping invitation to trouble surging up inside him. He fought it down and held himself still for an instant. Then he spoke.

"Reed, you're a fat-headed fool and a bully. You ride up here to take advantage of a woman because you think she's helpless. Well, she's not. Now you three turn your horses . . . turn 'em mighty careful . . . and start down the trail. And don't you ever set foot on this place again."

Reed's face went white, then dark with anger. He leaned forward a little. "So you're still here? Well, we'll give you a chance to run. Get goin'!"

Matt Sabre walked forward another step. He could feel the eagerness pushing up inside him, and his eyes held the three men, and he saw the eyes of one widen with apprehension.

134

"Watch it, boss! Watch it!"

"That's right, Reed. Watch it. You figured to find this girl alone. Well, she's not alone. Furthermore, if she'll take me on as a hand, I'll stay. I'll stay until you're out of the country or dead. You can have it either way you want. There's three of you. I like that. That evens us up. If you want to feed buzzards, just edge that hand another half inch toward your gun and you can. That goes for the three of you."

He stepped forward again. He was jumping with it now—that old drive for combat welling up within him. Inside, he was trembling, but his muscles were steady, and his mind was cool and ready. His fingers spread, and he moved forward again.

"Come on, you mangy coyotes. Let's see if you've got the nerve. Reach!"

Reed's face was still and cold. His mouth looked pinched, and his eyes were wide. Some sixth sense warned him that this was different. This was death he was looking at, and Galusha Reed suddenly realized he was no gambler when the stakes were so high.

He could see the dark eagerness that was driving this cool man; he could see beyond the coolness on his surface the fierceness of his readiness; inside, he went sick and cold at the thought.

"Boss," the man at his side whispered hoarsely, "let's get out of here. This man's poison."

Galusha Reed slowly eased his hand forward to the pommel of the saddle. "So, Jenny, you're hiring gunfighters? Is that the way you want it?"

"I think you hired them first," she replied coolly. "Now you'd better go."

"On the way back," Sabre suggested, "you might stop in Hardscrabble Cañon and pick up the body of one of your killers. He guessed wrong last night."

Reed stared at him. "I don't know what you mean!" he flared. "I sent out no killer."

Matt Sabre watched the three men ride down the trail and he frowned. There had been honest doubt in Reed's eyes, but if he had not sent the two men after him, who had? Those men had been in Silver City and El Paso, yet they also knew this country and knew someone in Yellow Jacket. Maybe they had not come after him but had first followed Bill Curtin.

He turned and smiled at the girl. "Coyotes," he said, shrugging. "Not much heart in them."

She was staring at him strangely. "You . . . you'd have killed them, wouldn't you? Why?"

He shrugged. "I don't know. Maybe it's because . . . well, I don't like to see men take advantage of a woman alone. Anyway"—he smiled—"Reed doesn't impress me as a good citizen."

"He's a dangerous enemy." She came down from the steps. "Did you mean what you said, Mister Sabre? I mean, about staying here and working for me? I need men, although I must tell you that you've small chance of winning, and it's rather a lonely fight."

"Yes, I meant it." Did he mean it? Of course. He remembered the old Chinese proverb: If you save a person's life, he becomes your responsibility. That wasn't the case here, but he had killed this girl's husband, and the least he could do would be to stay until she was out of trouble. Was that all he was thinking of? "I'll stay," he said. "I'll see you through this. I've been fighting all my life, and it would be a shame to stop now. And I've fought for lots less reasons."

III

Throughout the morning, he worked around the place. He worked partly because there was much to be done and partly because he wanted to think.

The horses in the remuda were held on the home place and were in good shape. Also, they were better than the usual ranch horses, for some of them showed a strong Morgan strain. He repaired the latch on the stable door and walked around the place, sizing it up from every angle, studying all the approaches.

With his glasses, he studied the hills and searched the notches and cañons wherever he could see them. Mentally he formed a map of all that terrain within reach of his glass.

It was mid-afternoon before Judson and Rado returned, and they had talked with Jenny before he saw them.

"Howdy." Judson was friendly, but his eyes studied Sabre with care. "Miz Jenny tells me you run Reed off. That you're aimin' to stay on here."

"That's right. I'll stay until she's out of trouble, if she'll have me. I don't like being pushed around."

"No, neither do I." Judson was silent for several moments, and then he turned his eyes on Sabre. "Don't you be gettin' any ideas about Miz Jenny. She's a fine girl."

Matt looked up angrily. "And don't you be getting any ideas," he said coldly. "I'm helping her the same as you are, and we'll work together. As to personal things, leave them alone. I'll only say that when this fight is over, I'm hitting the trail."

"All right," Judson said mildly. "We can use help."

Three days passed smoothly. Matt threw himself into the work of the ranch, and he worked feverishly. Even he could not have said why he worked so desperately hard. He dug post holes and fenced an area in the long meadow near the seeping springs in the bottom.

Then, working with Rado, he rounded up the cattle nearest the rim and pushed them back behind the fence. The grass was thick and deep there and would stand a lot of grazing, for the meadow wound back up the cañon for some distance. He carried a running iron and branded stock wherever he found it required.

As the ranch had been short-handed for a year, there was much to do. Evenings, he mended gear and worked around the place, and at night he slept soundly. During all this time, he saw nothing of Jenny Curtin.

He saw nothing of her, but she was constantly in his thoughts. He remembered her as he had seen her that first time, standing in the living room of the house, listening to him, her eyes, wide and dark, upon his face. He remembered her facing Galusha Reed and his riders from the steps.

Was he staying on because he believed he owed her a debt or because of her?

Here and there around the ranch, Sabre found small, intangible hints of the sort of man Curtin must have been. Judson had liked him, and so had the half-breed. He had been gentle with horses. He had been thoughtful. Yet he had hated and avoided violence. Slowly, rightly or wrongly Matt could not tell, a picture was forming in his mind of a fine young man who had been totally out of place.

Western by birth, but born for peaceful and quiet ways, he had been thrown into a cattle war and had been aware of his own inadequacy. Matt was thinking of that, and working at a rawhide reata, when Jenny came up.

He had not seen her approach, or he might have avoided her, but she was there beside him before he realized it.

"You're working hard, Mister Sabre."

"To earn my keep, ma'am. There's a lot to do, I find, and I like to keep busy." He turned the reata and studied it. "You know, there's something I've been wanting to talk to you about. Maybe it's none of my affair, but young Billy is going to grow up, and he's

139

going to ask questions about his dad. You aren't going to be able to fool him. Maybe you know what this is all about, and maybe I'm mounting on the off-side, but it seems to me that Bill Curtin went to El Paso to get that money for you.

"I think he realized he was no fighting man, and that the best thing he could do was to get that money so he could hire gunfighters. It took nerve to do what he did, and I think he deliberately took what Sikes handed him because he knew that, if Sikes killed him, you'd never get that money.

"Maybe along the way to El Paso he began to wonder, and maybe he picked that fight down there with the idea of proving to himself that he did have the nerve to face a gun."

She did not reply, but stood there, watching his fingers work swiftly and evenly, plaiting the leather.

"Yes," she said finally, "I thought of that. Only I can't imagine where he got the money. I hesitate to use it without knowing."

"Don't be foolish," he said irritably. "Use it. Nobody would put it to better use, and you need gun hands."

"But who would work for me?" Her voice was low and bitter. "Galusha Reed has seen to it that no one will."

"Maybe if I rode in, I could find some men." He was thinking of Camp Gordon, the Shakespeare-quoting English cowhand. "I believe I know one man."

140

"There's a lot to be done. Jud tells me you've been doing the work of three men."

Matt Sabre got to his feet. She stepped back a little, suddenly aware of how tall he was. She was tall for a girl, yet she came no farther than his lips. She drew back a little at the thought. Her eyes dropped to his guns. He always wore them, always low and tied-down.

"Judson said you were a fast man with a gun. He said you had the mark of the . . . of the gunfighter."

"Probably." He found no bitterness at the thought. "I've used guns. Guns and horses, they are about all I've known."

"Where were you in the army? I've watched you walk and ride and you show military training."

"Oh, several places. Africa mostly."

"Africa?" She was amazed. "You've been there?"

He nodded. "Desert and mountain country. Morocco and the Sahara, all the way to Timbuktu and Lake Chad, fighting most of the time." It was growing dark in the shed where they were standing. He moved out into the dusk. A few stars had already appeared, and the red glow that was in the west beyond the rim was fading.

"Tomorrow I'll ride in and have a look around. You'd better keep the other men close by."

Dawn found him well along on the trail to Yellow Jacket. It was a long ride, and he skirted the trail most of the time, having no trust in well-traveled

141

ways at such a time. The air was warm and bright, and he noticed a few head of Pivotrock steers that had been overlooked in the rounding up of cattle along the rim.

He rode ready for trouble, his Winchester across his saddle bows, his senses alert. Keeping the roan well back under the trees, he had the benefit of the evergreen needles that formed a thick carpet and muffled the sound of his horse's hoofs.

Yet, as he rode, he considered the problem of the land grant. If Jenny were to retain her land and be free of trouble, he must look into the background of the grant and see which had the prior and best claim, Fernandez or Sonoma.

Next, he must find out, if possible, where Bill Curtin had obtained that $5,000. Some might think that the fact he had it was enough and that now his wife had it, but it was not enough if Bill had sold any rights to water or land on the ranch or if he had obtained the money in some way that would reflect upon Jenny or her son.

When those things were done, he could ride on about his business, for by that time he would have worked out the problem of Galusha Reed.

In the few days he had been on the Pivotrock, he had come to love the place, and, while he had avoided Jenny, he had not avoided young Billy. The youngster had adopted him and had stayed with him hour after hour.

To keep him occupied, Matt had begun teaching

him how to plait rawhide, and so, as he mended reatas and repaired bridles, the youngster had sat beside him, working his fingers clumsily through the intricacies of the plaiting.

It was with unease that he recalled his few minutes alone with Jenny. He shifted his seat in the saddle and scowled. It would not do for him to think of her as anything but Curtin's widow. The widow, he reflected bitterly, of the man he had killed.

What would he say when she learned of that? He avoided the thought, yet it remained in the back of his mind, and he shook his head, wanting to forget it. Sooner or later, she would know. If he did not finally tell her himself, then he was sure that Reed would let her know.

Avoiding the route by way of Hardscrabble, Matt Sabre turned due south, crossing the eastern end of the mesa and following an old trail across Whiterock and Polles Mesa, crossing the East Verde at Rock Creek. Then he cut through Boardinghouse Cañon to Bullspring, crossing the main stream of the Verde near Tangle Peak. It was a longer way around by a few miles, but Sabre rode with care, watching the country as he traveled. It was very late when he walked his roan into the parched street of Yellow Jacket.

He had a hunch and he meant to follow it through. During his nights in the bunkhouse he had talked much with Judson, and from him heard of Pepito Fernandez, a grandson of the man who sold the land to Old Man Curtin.

Swinging down from his horse at the livery stable, he led him inside. Simpson walked over to meet him, his eyes searching Sabre's face. "Man, you've a nerve with you. Reed's wild. He came back to town blazing mad, and Trumbull's telling everybody what you can expect."

Matt smiled at the man. "I expected that. Where do you stand?"

"Well," Simpson said grimly, "I've no liking for Trumbull. He carries himself mighty big around town, and he's not been friendly to me and mine. I reckon, mister, I've rare been so pleased as when you made a fool of him in yonder. It was better than the killing of him, although he's that coming, sure enough."

"Then take care of my horse, will you? And a slip-knot to tie him with."

"Sure, and he'll get corn, too. I reckon any horse you ride would need corn."

Matt Sabre walked out on the street. He was wearing dark jeans and a gray wool shirt. His black hat was pulled low, and he merged well with the shadows. He'd see Pepito first, and then look around a bit. He wanted Camp Gordon.

Thinking of that, he turned back into the stable. "Saddle Gordon's horse, too. He'll be going back with me."

"Him?" Simpson stared. "Man, he's dead drunk and has been for days!"

"Saddle his horse. He'll be with me when I'm

back, and, if you know another one or two good hands who would use a gun if need be, let them know I'm hiring and there's money to pay them. Fighting wages if they want."

In the back office of the Yellow Jacket, three men sat around Galusha Reed's desk. There was Reed himself, Sid Trumbull, and Prince McCarran.

"Do you think Tony can take him?" Reed asked. "You've seen the man draw, Prince."

"He'll take him. But it will be close . . . too close. I think what we'd better do is have Sid posted somewhere close by."

"Leave me out of it." Sid looked up from under his thick eyebrows. "I want no more of the man. Let Tony have him."

"You won't be in sight," McCarran said dryly, "or in danger. You'll be upstairs over the hotel, with a Winchester."

Trumbull looked up and touched his thick lips with his tongue. Killing was not new to him, yet the way this man accepted it always appalled him a little.

"All right," he agreed. "Like I say, I've no love for him."

"We'll have him so you'll get a flanking shot. Make it count and make it the first time. But wait until the shooting starts."

The door opened softly, and Sikes stepped in. He was a lithe, dark-skinned man who moved like an animal. He had graceful hands, restless hands. He

145

wore a white buckskin vest worked with red quills and beads. "Boss, he's in town. Sabre's here." He had heard them.

Reed let his chair legs down, leaning forward. "Here? In town?"

"That's right. I just saw him outside the Yellow Jacket." Sikes started to build a cigarette. "He's got nerve. Plenty of it."

The door sounded with a light tap, and at a word Keys entered. He was a slight man with gray hair and a quiet scholar's face.

"I remember him now, Prince," he said. "Matt Sabre. I'd been trying to place the name. He was marshal of Mobeetie for a while. He's killed eight or nine men."

"That's right!" Trumbull looked up sharply. "Mobeetie! Why didn't I remember that? They say Wes Hardin rode out of town once when Sabre sent him word he wasn't wanted."

Sikes turned his eyes on McCarran. "You want him now?"

McCarran hesitated, studying the polished toe of his boot. Sabre's handling of Trumbull had made friends in town, and also his championing of the cause of Jenny Curtin. Whatever happened must be seemingly aboveboard and in the clear, and he wanted to be where he could be seen at the time, and Reed, also.

"No, not now. We'll wait." He smiled. "One thing about a man of his courage and background, if you send for him, he'll always come to you."

"But how will he come?" Keys asked softly. "That's the question."

McCarran looked around irritably. He had forgotten Keys was in the room and had said far more than he had intended. "Thanks, Keys. That will be all. And remember . . . nothing will be said about anything you've heard here."

"Certainly not." Keys smiled and walked to the door and out of the room.

Reed stared after him. "I don't like that fellow, Prince. I wouldn't trust him."

"Him? He's interested in nothing but that piano and enough liquor to keep himself mildly embalmed. Don't worry about him."

IV

Matt Sabre turned away from the Yellow Jacket after a brief survey of the saloon. Obviously something was doing elsewhere for none of the men was present in the big room. He hesitated, considering the significance of that, and then turned down a dark alleyway and walked briskly along until he came to an old rail fence.

Following this past rustling cottonwoods and down a rutted road, he turned past a barn and cut across another road toward an adobe where the windows glowed with a faint light.

The door opened to his knock, and a dark, Indian-like face showed briefly. In rapid Spanish he asked for Pepito. After a moment's hesitation, the door widened, and he was invited inside.

The room was large, and at one side a small fire burned in the blackened fireplace. An oilcloth-covered table with a coal-oil light stood in the middle of the room, and on a bed at one side a man snored peacefully.

A couple of dark-eyed children ceased their playing to look up at him. The woman called out, and a blanket pushed aside, and a slender, dark-faced youth entered the room, pulling his belt tight.

"Pepito Fernandez? I am Matt Sabre."

"I have heard of you, *señor*."

Briefly he explained why he had come, and Pepito listened, then shook his head. "I do not know, *señor*. The grant was long ago, and we are no longer rich. My father"—he shrugged—"he liked the spending of money when he was young." He hesitated, considering that. Then he said carelessly: "I, too, like the spending of money. What else is it for? But no, *señor*, I do not think there are papers. My father, he told me much of the grant, and I am sure the Sonomas had no strong claim."

"If you remember anything, will you let us know?" Sabre asked. Then a thought occurred to him. "You're a *vaquero*? Do you want a job?"

"A job?" Pepito studied him thoughtfully. "At the *Señora* Curtin's ranch?"

"Yes. As you know, there may be much trouble. I am working there, and tonight I shall take one other

148

man back with me. If you would like the job, it is yours."

Pepito shrugged. "Why not? *Señor* Curtin, the old one, he gave me my first horse. He gave me a rifle, too. He was a good one, and the son, also."

"Better meet me outside of town where the trail goes between the buttes. You know the place?"

"*Sí, señor*. I will be there."

Keys was idly playing the piano when Matt Sabre opened the door and stepped into the room. His quick eyes placed Keys, Hobbs at the bar, Camp Gordon fast asleep with his head on a table, and a half dozen other men. Yet, as he walked to the bar, a rear door opened, and Tony Sikes stepped into the room.

Sabre had never before seen the man, yet he knew him from Judson's apt and careful description. Sikes was not as tall as Sabre, yet more slender. He had the wiry, stringy build that is made for speed and quick, smooth-flowing fingers. His muscles were relaxed and easy, but knowing such men Matt recognized danger when he saw it. Sikes had seen him at once, and he moved to the bar nearby.

All eyes were on the two of them, for the story of Matt's whipping of Trumbull and his defiance of Reed had swept the country. Yet Sikes merely smiled and Matt glanced at him. "Have a drink?"

Tony Sikes nodded. "I don't mind if I do." Then he added, his voice low and his dark, yellowish eyes on

Matt's with a faintly sardonic, faintly amused look: "I never mind drinking with a man I'm going to kill."

Sabre shrugged. "Neither do I." He found himself liking Sikes's direct approach. "Although perhaps I have the advantage. I choose my own time to drink and to kill. You wait for orders."

Tony Sikes felt in his vest pocket for cigarette papers and began to roll a smoke. "You will wait for me, *compadre*. I know you're the type."

They drank, and, as they drank, the door opened, and Galusha Reed stepped out. His face darkened angrily when he saw the two standing at the bar together, but he was passing without speaking when a thought struck him. He stopped and turned.

"I wonder," he said loudly enough for all in the room to hear, "what Jenny Curtin will say when she finds out her new hand is the man who killed her husband?"

Every head came up, and Sabre's face whitened. Whereas the faces had been friendly or non-committal, now they were sharp-eyed and attentive. Moreover, he knew that Jenny was well liked, as Curtin had been. Now they would be his enemies.

"I wonder just why you came here, Sabre? After killing the girl's husband, why would you come to her ranch? Was it to profit from your murder? To steal what little she has left? Or is it for the girl herself?"

Matt struggled to keep his temper. After a minute, he said casually: "Reed, it was you ordered her off her ranch. I'm here for one reason, and one alone. To see that she keeps her ranch and that no yellow-bellied, thievin' lot of coyotes ride over and take it away from her."

Reed stood flat-footed, facing Sabre. He was furious, and Matt could feel the force of his rage. It was almost a physical thing pushing against him. Close beside him was Sikes. If Reed chose to go for a gun, Sikes could grab Matt's left arm and jerk him off balance. Yet Matt was ready even for that, and again that black force was rising within him, that driving urge toward violence.

He spoke again, and his voice was soft and almost purring. "Make up your mind, Reed. If you want to die, you can right here. You make another remark to me and I'll drive every word of it back down that fat throat of yours. Reach, and I'll kill you. If Sikes wants in on this, he's welcome."

Tony Sikes spoke softly, too. "I'm out of it, Sabre. I only fight my own battles. When I come after you, I'll be alone."

Galusha Reed hesitated. For an instant, counting on Sikes, he had been tempted. Now he hesitated, then turned abruptly and left the room.

Ignoring Sikes, Sabre downed his drink and crossed to Camp Gordon. He shook him. "Come on, Camp. I'm puttin' you to bed."

Gordon did not move. Sabre stooped and slipped an arm around the big Englishman's shoulders and, hoisting him to his feet, started for the door. At the

151

door, he turned. "I'll be seeing you, Sikes."

Tony lifted his glass, his hat pushed back. "Sure," he said. "And I'll be alone."

It was not until after he had said it that he remembered Sid Trumbull and the plans made in the back room. His face darkened a little, and his liquor suddenly tasted badly. He put his glass down carefully on the bar and turned, walking through the back door.

Prince McCarran was alone, idly riffling the cards and smoking. "I won't do it, Prince," Sikes said. "You've got to leave that killing to me and me alone."

Matt Sabre, with Camp Gordon lashed to the saddle of a led horse, met Pepito in the darkness of the space between the buttes. Pepito spoke softly, and Sabre called back to him. As the Mexican rode out, he glanced once at Gordon, and then the three rode on together. It was late the following morning when they reached the Pivotrock.

Camp Gordon was sober and swearing. "Shanghaied!" His voice exploded with violence. "You've a nerve, Sabre. Turn me loose so I can start back. I'm having no part of this."

Gordon was tied to his horse so he would not fall off, but Matt only grinned. "Sure, I'll turn you loose. But you said you ought to get out of town a while, and this was the best way. I've brought you here," he said gravely, but his eyes were twinkling, "for your own good. It's time you had some fresh, mountain air, some cold milk, some. . . ."

"Milk?" Gordon exploded. "Milk, you say? I'll not touch the stuff! Turn me loose and give me a gun and I'll have your hide!"

"And leave this ranch for Reed to take? Reed and McCarran?"

Gordon stared at him from bloodshot eyes, eyes that were suddenly attentive. "Did you say McCarran? What's he got to do with this?"

"I wish I knew. But I've a hunch he's in up to his ears. I think he has strings on Reed."

Gordon considered that. "He may have." He watched Sabre undoing the knots. "It's a point I hadn't considered. But why?"

"You've known him longer than I have. Somebody had two men follow Curtin out of the country to kill him, and I don't believe Reed did it. Does that make sense?"

"No." Gordon swung stiffly to the ground. He swayed a bit, clinging to the stirrup leather. He glanced sheepishly at Matt. "I guess I'm a mess." A surprised look crossed his face. "Say, I'm hungry! I haven't been hungry in weeks."

With four hands besides himself, work went on swiftly. Yet Matt Sabre's mind would not rest. The $5,000 was a problem, and also there was the grant. Night after night, he led Pepito to talk of the memories of his father and grandfather, and little by little he began to know the men. An idea was shaping in his mind, but as yet there was little on which to build.

In all this time, there was no sign of Reed. On two occasions, riders had been seen, apparently scouting. Cattle had been swept from the rim edge and pushed back, accounting for all or nearly all the strays he had seen on his ride to Yellow Jacket.

Matt was restless, sure that when trouble came, it would come with a rush. It was like Reed to do things that way. By now he was certainly aware that Camp Gordon and Pepito Fernandez had been added to the roster of hands at Pivotrock.

"Spotted a few head over near Baker Butte," Camp said one morning. "How'd it be if I drifted that way and looked them over?"

"We'll go together," Matt replied. "I've been wanting to look around there, and there's been no chance."

The morning was bright, and they rode swiftly, putting miles behind them, alert to all the sights and sounds of the high country above the rim. Careful as they were, they were no more than 100 yards from the riders when they saw them. There were five men, and in the lead rode Sid Trumbull and a white-mustached stranger.

There was no possibility of escaping unnoticed. They pushed on toward the advancing riders, who drew up and waited. Sid Trumbull's face was sharp with triumph when he saw Sabre.

154

"Here's your man, Marshal!" he said with satisfaction. "The one with the black hat is Sabre."

"What's this all about?" Matt asked quietly. He had already noticed the badge the man wore. But he noticed something else. The man looked to be a competent, upstanding officer.

"You're wanted in El Paso. I'm Rafe Collins, deputy United States marshal. We're making an inquiry into the killing of Bill Curtin."

Camp's lips tightened, and he looked sharply at Sabre. When Reed had brought out this fact in the saloon, Gordon had been dead drunk.

"That was a fair shooting, Marshal. Curtin picked the fight and drew on me."

"You expect us to believe that?" Trumbull was contemptuous. "Why, he hadn't the courage of a mouse! He backed down from Sikes only a few days before. He wouldn't draw on any man with two hands!"

"He drew on me." Matt Sabre realized he was fighting two battles here—one to keep from being arrested, the other to keep Gordon's respect and assistance. "My idea is that he only backed out of a fight with Sikes because he had a job to do and knew Sikes would kill him."

"That's a likely yarn!" Trumbull nodded. "There's your man. It's your job, Marshal."

Collins was obviously irritated. That he entertained no great liking for Trumbull was obvious. Yet he had his duty to do. Before he could speak, Sabre spoke again.

"Marshal, I've reason to believe that some influence has been brought to bear to discredit me and to get me out of the country for a while. Can't I give you my word that I'll report to El Paso when things are straightened out? My word is good, and there are many in El Paso who know that."

"Sorry." Collins was regretful. "I've my duty and my orders."

"I understand that," Sabre replied. "I also have my duty. It is to see that Jenny Curtin is protected from those who are trying to force her off her range. I intend to do exactly that."

"Your duty?" Collins eyed him coldly but curiously. "After killing her husband?"

"That's reason enough, sir," Sabre replied flatly. "The fight was not my choice. Curtin pushed it, and he was excited, worried, and overwrought. Yet he asked me on his deathbed to deliver a package to his wife and to see that she was protected. That duty, sir"—his eyes met those of Collins—"comes first."

"I'd like to respect that," Collins admitted. "You seem like a gentleman, sir, and it's a quality that's too rare. Unfortunately I have my orders. However, it should not take long to straighten this out if it was a fair shooting."

"All these rats need," Sabre replied, "is a few days." He knew there was no use arguing. His horse was fast, and dense pines bordered the road. He needed a minute, and that badly.

As if divining his thought, Camp Gordon suddenly

156

pushed his gray between Matt and the marshal, and almost at once Matt lashed out with his toe and booted Trumbull's horse in the ribs. The bronco went to bucking furiously. Whipping his horse around, Matt slapped the spurs to his ribs, and in two startled jumps he was off and deep into the pines, running like a startled deer.

Behind him a shot rang out, and then another. Both cut the brush over his head, but the horse was running now, and he was mounted well. He had started into the trees at right angles but swung his horse immediately and headed back toward the Pivotrock. Corduroy Wash opened off to his left, and he turned the black and pushed rapidly into the mouth of the wash.

Following it for almost a mile, he came out and paused briefly in the clump of trees that crowned a small ridge. He stared back.

A string of riders stretched out on his back trail, but they were scattered out, hunting for tracks. A lone horseman sat not far from them, obviously watching. Matt grinned. That would be Gordon, and he was all right.

Turning his horse, Matt followed a shelf of rock until it ran out, rode off it into thick sand, and then into the pines with their soft bed of needles that left almost no tracks.

Cinch Hook Butte was off to his left, and nearer, on his right, Twenty-Nine-Mile Butte. Keeping his horse headed between them, but bearing steadily northwest, he headed for the broken country around Horsetank Wash. Descending into the cañon, he rode northwest, then circled back south, and entered the even deeper Calfpen Cañon.

Here, in a nest of boulders, he staked out his horse on a patch of grass. Rifle across his knees, he rested. After an hour, he worked his way to the ledge at the top of the cañon, but nowhere could he see any sign of pursuit. Nor could he hear the sound of hoofs.

There was water in the bottom of Calfpen, not far from where he had left his horse. Food was something else again. He shucked a handful of chia seeds and ate a handful of them, along with the nuts of a piñon.

Obviously the attempted arrest had been brought about by either the influence of Galusha Reed or Prince McCarran. In either case, he was now a fugitive. If they went on to the ranch, Rafe Collins would have a chance to talk to Jenny Curtin. Matt felt sick when he thought of the marshal telling her that it was he who had killed her husband. That she must find out sooner or later, he knew, but he wanted to tell her himself, in his own good time.

V

When dusk had fallen, he mounted the black and worked his way down Calfpen toward Fossil Springs. As he rode, he was considering his best course. Whether taken by Collins or not, he was not now at the ranch and they might choose this time to strike. With some reason, they might believe he had left the country. Indeed, there was every chance that Reed actually believed he had come there with some plan of his own to get the Curtin ranch.

Finally he bedded down for the night in a draw above Fossil Springs and slept soundly until daylight brought a sun that crept over the rocks and shone upon his eyes. He was up, made a light breakfast of coffee and jerked beef, and then saddled up.

Wherever he went now, he could expect hostility. Doubt or downright suspicion would have developed as a result of Reed's accusation in Yellow Jacket, and the country would know the U.S. marshal was looking for him.

Debating his best course, Matt Sabre headed west through the mountains. By nightfall the following day, he was camped in the ominous shadow of Turret Butte where only a few years before Major Randall had ascended the peak in darkness to surprise a camp of Apaches.

Awakening at the break of dawn, Matt scouted the vicinity of Yellow Jacket with care.

There was some movement in town—more than usual at that hour. He observed a long line of saddled horses at the hitch rails. He puzzled over this, studying it with narrowed eyes from the crest of a ridge through his glasses. Marshal Collins could not yet have returned, hence this must be some other movement. That it was organized was obvious.

He was still watching when a man wearing a faded red shirt left the back door of a building near the saloon, went to a horse carefully hidden in the rear, and mounted. At this distance, there was no way of seeing who he was. The man rode strangely. Studying him through the glasses—a relic of Sabre's military years—Matt suddenly realized why the rider seemed strange. He was riding Eastern fashion!

This was no Westerner, slouched and lazy in the saddle, nor yet sitting upright as a cavalryman might. This man rode forward on his horse, a poor practice for the hard miles of desert or mountain riding. Yet it was his surreptitious manner rather than his riding style that intrigued Matt. It required but a few minutes for Matt to see that the route the rider was taking away from town would bring him by near the base of the promontory where he watched.

Reluctant as he was to give over watching the saddled horses, Sabre was sure this strange rider held some clue to his problems. Sliding back on his belly well into the brush, Matt got to his feet and descended the steep trail and took up his place among the boulders beside the trail.

It was very hot there out of the breeze, yet he had waited only a minute until he heard the sound of the approaching horse. He cleared his gun from its holster and moved to the very edge of the road. Then the rider appeared. It was Keys.

Matt's gun stopped him. "Where you ridin', Keys?" Matt asked quietly. "What's this all about?"

"I'm riding to intercept the marshal," Keys said sincerely. "McCarran and Reed plan to send out a posse of their own men to hunt you, then, under cover of capturing you, they intend to take the Pivotrock and hold it."

Sabre nodded. That would be it, of course, and he should have guessed it before. "What about the marshal? They'll run into him on the trail."

"No, they're going to swing south of his trail. They know how he's riding because Reed is guiding him."

"What's your stake in this? Why ride all the way out there to tell the marshal?"

"It's because of Jenny Curtin," he said frankly. "She's a fine girl, and Bill was a good boy. Both of them treated me fine, as their father did before them. It's little enough to do, and I know too much about the plotting of that devil McCarran."

"Then it is McCarran. Where does Reed stand in this?"

"He's stupid," Keys said contemptuously. "McCarran is using him, and he hasn't the wit to see it. He believes they are partners, but Prince will get rid of him like he does anyone who gets in his way. He'll be rid of Trumbull, too."

"And Sikes?"

"Perhaps. Sikes is a good tool, to a point."

Matt Sabre shoved his hat back on his head. "Keys," he said suddenly, "I want you to have a little faith in me. Believe me, I'm doing what I can to help Jenny Curtin. I did kill her husband, but he was a total stranger who was edgy and started a fight.

"I'd no way of knowing who or what he was, and the gun of a stranger kills as easy as the gun of a known man. But he trusted me. He asked me to come here, to bring his wife five thousand, and to help her."

"Five thousand?" Keys stared. "Where did he get that amount of money?"

"I'd like to know," Sabre admitted. Another idea occurred to him. "Keys, you know more about what's going on in this town than anyone else. What do you know about the Sonoma Grant?"

Keys hesitated, then said slowly: "Sabre, I know very little about that. I think the only one who has the true facts is Prince McCarran. I think he gathered all the available papers on both grants and is sure that no matter what his claim, the grant cannot be substantiated. Nobody knows but McCarran."

"Then I'll go to McCarran," Sabre replied harshly. "I'm going to straighten this out if it's the last thing I do."

"You go to McCarran and it will be the last thing you do. The man's deadly. He's smooth-talking and treacherous. And then there's Sikes."

"Yes," Sabre admitted. "There's Sikes." He studied the situation, then looked up. "Don't you bother the marshal. Leave him to me. Every man he's got with him is an enemy to Jenny Curtin, and they would never let you talk. You circle them and ride on to Pivotrock. You tell Camp Gordon what's happening.

Tell him of this outfit that's saddled up. I'll do my job here, and then I'll start back."

Long after Keys had departed, Sabre watched. Evidently the posse was awaiting some word from Reed. Would McCarran ride with them? He was too careful. He would wait in Yellow Jacket. He would be, as always, an innocent bystander. . . .

Keys, riding up the trail some miles distant, drew up suddenly. He had forgotten to tell Sabre of Prince McCarran's plan to have Sid Trumbull cut him down when he tangled with Sikes. For a long moment, Keys sat his horse, staring worriedly and scowling. To go back now would lose time; moreover, there was small chance that Sabre would be there. Matt Sabre would have to take his own chances.

Regretfully Keys pushed on into the rough country ahead. . . .

Tony Sikes found McCarran seated in the back room at the saloon. McCarran glanced up quickly as he came in, and then nodded.

"Glad to see you, Sikes. I want you close by. I think we'll have visitors today or tomorrow."

"Visitors?" Sikes searched McCarran's face.

"A visitor, I should say. I think we'll see Matt Sabre."

Tony Sikes considered that, turning it over in his mind. Yes, Prince was right. Sabre would not surrender. It would be like him to head for town,

163

hunting Reed. Aside from three or four men, nobody knew of McCarran's connection with the Pivotrock affair. Reed and Trumbull were fronting for him.

Trumbull, Reed, Sikes, and Keys. Keys was a shrewd man. He might be a drunk and a piano player, but he had a head on his shoulders.

Sikes's mind leaped suddenly. Keys was not around. This was the first time in weeks that he had not encountered Keys in the bar.

Keys was gone.

Where would he go—to warn Jenny Curtin of the posse? So what? He had nothing against Jenny Curtin. He was a man who fought for hire. Maybe he was on the wrong side in this. Even as he thought of that, he remembered Matt Sabre. The man was sharp as a steel blade—trim, fast. Now that it had been recalled to his mind, he remembered all that he had heard of him as marshal of Mobeetie.

There was in Tony Sikes a drive that forbade him to admit any man was his fighting superior. Sabre's draw against Trumbull was still the talk of the town—talk that irked Sikes, for folks were beginning to compare the two of them. Many thought Sabre might be faster. That rankled.

He would meet Sabre first and then drift.

"Don't you think he'll get here?" McCarran asked, looking up at Tony.

Sikes nodded. "He'll get here, all right. He thinks too fast for Trumbull or Reed. Even for that marshal."

164

Sikes would have Sabre to himself. Sid Trumbull was out of town. Tony Sikes wanted to do his own killing.

Matt Sabre watched the saddled horses. He had that quality of patience so long associated with the Indian. He knew how to wait and how to relax. He waited now, letting all his muscles rest. With all his old alertness for danger—his sixth sense that warned him of climaxes—he knew this situation had reached the explosion point.

The marshal would be returning. Reed and Trumbull would be sure that he did not encounter the posse. And that body of riders, most of whom were henchmen or cronies of Galusha Reed, would sweep down on the Pivotrock and capture it, killing all who were there under the pretense of searching for Matt Sabre.

Keys would warn them, and in time. Once they knew of the danger, Camp Gordon and the others would be wise enough to take the necessary precautions. The marshal was one tentacle, but there in Yellow Jacket was the heart of the trouble.

If Prince McCarran and Tony Sikes were removed, the tentacles would shrivel and die. Despite the danger out at Pivotrock, high behind the Mogollon Rim, the decisive blow must be struck right here in Yellow Jacket.

He rolled over on his stomach and lifted the glasses. Men were coming from the Yellow Jacket

Saloon and mounting up. Lying at his ease, he watched them go. There were at least thirty, possibly more. When they had gone, he got to his feet and brushed off his clothes. Then he walked slowly down to his horse and mounted.

He rode quietly, one hand lying on his thigh, his eyes alert, his brain relaxed and ready for impressions.

Marshal Rafe Collins was a just man. He was a frontiersman, a man who knew the West and the men it bred. He was no fool—shrewd and careful, rigid in his enforcement of the law, yet wise in the ways of men. Moreover, he was Southern in the oldest of Southern traditions, and, being so, he understood what Matt Sabre meant when he said it was because he had killed her husband that he must protect Jenny Curtin.

Matt Sabre left his horse at the livery stable. Simpson looked up sharply when he saw him.

"You better watch yourself," he warned. "The whole country's after you, an' they are huntin' blood!"

"I know. What about Sikes? Is he in town?"

"Sure! He never leaves McCarran." Simpson searched his face. "Sikes is no man to tangle with, Sabre. He's chain lightnin'."

"I know." Sabre watched his horse led into a shadowed stall. Then he turned to Simpson. "You've been friendly, Simpson. I like that. After today, there's goin' to be a new order of things around here, but today I could use some help. What do you know about the Pivotrock deal?"

The man hesitated, chewing slowly. Finally he spat and looked up. "There was nobody to tell until now," he said, "but two things I know. That grant was Curtin's, all right, an' he wasn't killed by accident. He was murdered."

"Murdered?"

"Yeah." Simpson's expression was wry. "Like you he liked fancy drinkin' liquor when he could get it. McCarran was right friendly. He asked Curtin to have a drink with him that day, an' Curtin did.

"On'y a few minutes after that, he came in here an' got a team to drive back, leavin' his horse in here because it had gone lame. I watched him climb into that rig, an' he missed the step an' almost fell on his face. Then he finally managed to climb in."

"Drunk?" Sabre's eyes were alert and interested.

"Him?" Simpson snorted. "That old coot could stow away more liquor than a turkey could corn. He had only one drink, yet he could hardly walk."

"Doped, then?" Sabre nodded. That sounded like McCarran. "And then what?"

"When the team was brought back after they ran away with him, an' after Curtin was found dead, I found a bullet graze on the hip of one of those bronc's."

So that was how it had been. A doped man, a skittish team of horses, and a bullet to burn the horse just enough to start it running. Prince McCarran was a thorough man.

167

"You said you knew that Curtin really owned that grant. How?"

Simpson shrugged. "Because he had that other claim investigated. He must have heard rumors of trouble. There'd been talk of it that I heard, an' here a man hears everythin'!

"Anyway, he had all the papers with him when he started back to the ranch that day. He showed 'em to me earlier. All the proof."

"And he was murdered that day? Who found the body?"

"Sid Trumbull. He was ridin' that way, sort of accidental like."

The proof Jenny needed was in the hands of Prince McCarran. By all means, he must call on Prince.

VI

Matt Sabre walked to the door and stood there, waiting a moment in the shadow before emerging into the sunlight.

The street was dusty and curiously empty. The rough-fronted gray buildings of unpainted lumber or sand-colored adobe faced him blankly from across and up the street. The hitch rail was deserted; the water trough overflowed a little, making a darkening stain under one end.

Somewhere up the street, but behind the buildings, a hen began proclaiming her egg to the hemispheres. A single white cloud hung lazily in the blue sky. Matt stepped out. Hitching his gun belts a little, he looked up the street.

Sikes would be in the Yellow Jacket. To see McCarran, he must see Sikes first. That was the way he wanted it. One thing at a time.

He was curiously quiet. He thought of other times when he had faced such situations—of Mobeetie, of that first day out on the plains hunting buffalo, of the first time he had killed a man, of a charge the Riffs had made on a small desert patrol out of Taudeni long ago.

A faint breeze stirred an old sack that lay near the boardwalk, and farther up the street, near the water trough, a long gray rat slipped out from under a store and headed toward the drip of water from the trough. Matt Sabre started to walk, moving up the street.

It was not far, as distance goes, but there is no walk as long as the gunman's walk, no pause as long as the pause before gunfire. On this day, Sikes would know, instantly, what his presence here presaged. McCarran would know, too.

Prince McCarran was not a gambler. He would scarcely trust all to Tony Sikes no matter how confident he might be. It always paid to have something to back up a facing card. Trust Prince to keep his hole card well covered. But on this occasion, he would not be bluffing. He would have a hole card, but where? How? What? And when?

The last was not hard. When—the moment of the gun battle.

169

He had walked no more than thirty yards when a door *creaked* and a man stepped into the street. He did not look down toward Sabre but walked briskly to the center of the street, then faced about sharply like a man on a parade ground.

Tony Sikes.

He wore this day a faded blue shirt that stretched tightly over his broad, bony shoulders and fell slackly in front where his chest was hollow and his stomach flat. It was too far yet to see his eyes, but Matt Sabre knew what they looked like.

The thin, angular face, the mustache, the high cheek bones, and the long, restless fingers. The man's hips were narrow, and there was little enough to his body. Tony Sikes lifted his eyes and stared down the street. His lips were dry, but he felt ready. There was a curious lightness within him, but he liked it so, and he liked the set-up. At that moment, he felt almost an affection for Sabre.

The man knew so well the rules of the game. He was coming as he should come, and there was something about him—an edged quality, a poised and alert strength.

No sound penetrated the clear globe of stillness. The warm air hung still, with even the wind poised, arrested by the drama in the street. Matt Sabre felt a slow trickle of sweat start from under his hatband. He walked carefully, putting each foot down with care and distinction of purpose. It was Tony Sikes who stopped first, some sixty yards away.

"Well, Matt, here it is. We both knew it was coming."

"Sure." Matt paused, too, feet apart, hands swinging widely. "You tied up with the wrong outfit, Sikes."

"We'd have met, anyway." Sikes looked along the street at the tall man standing there, looked and saw his bronzed face, hard and ready. It was not in Sikes to feel fear of a man with guns. Yet this was how he would die. It was in the cards. He smiled suddenly. Yes, he would die by the gun—but not now.

His hands stirred, and, as if their movement was a signal to his muscles, they flashed in a draw. Before him, the dark, tall figure flashed suddenly. It was no more than that, a blur of movement and a lifted gun, a movement suddenly stilled, and the black sullen muzzle of a six-gun that steadied on him even as he cleared his gun from his open top holster.

He had been beaten—beaten to the draw.

The shock of it triggered Sikes's gun, and he knew even as the gun bucked in his hand that he had missed, and then suddenly Matt Sabre was running! Running toward him, gun lifted, but not firing!

In a panic, Sikes saw the distance closing and he fired as fast as he could pull the trigger, three times in a thundering cascade of sound. And even as the hammer fell for the fourth shot, he heard another gun bellow.

But where? There had been no stab of flame from Sabre's gun. Sabre was running, a rapidly moving target, and Sikes had fired too fast, upset by the sudden rush, by the panic of realizing he had been beaten to the draw.

He lifted his right-hand gun, dropped the muzzle in a careful arc, and saw Sabre's skull over the barrel. Then Sabre skidded to a halt, and his gun hammered bullets.

Flame leaped from the muzzle, stabbing at Sikes, burning him along the side, making his body twitch and the bullet go wild. He switched guns, and then something slugged him in the wind, and the next he knew he was on the ground.

Matt Sabre had heard that strange shot, but that was another thing. He could not wait now; he could not turn his attention. He saw Sikes go down, but only to his knees, and the gunman had five bullets and the range now was only fifteen yards.

Sikes's gun swung up, and Matt fired again. Sikes lunged to his feet, and then his features writhed with agony and breathlessness, and he went down, hard to the ground, twisting in the dust.

Then another bullet bellowed, and a shot kicked up dust at his feet. Matt swung his gun and blasted at an open window, then started for the saloon door. He stopped, hearing a loud cry behind him.

"Matt Sabre?"

It was Sikes, his eyes flared widely. Sabre hesitated, glanced swiftly around, then dropped to his knees in the silent street.

"What is it, Tony? Anything I can do for you?"

172

"Behind . . . behind . . . the desk . . . you . . . you. . . ."
His faltering voice faded, then strength seemed to flood
back, and he looked up. "Good man! Too . . . too fast!"

And then he was dead, gone just like that, and Matt
Sabre was striding into the Yellow Jacket.

The upstairs room was empty; the stairs were
empty; there was no one in sight. Only Hobbs stood
behind the bar when he came down. Hobbs, his face
set and pale.

Sabre looked at him, eyes steady and cold. "Who
came down those stairs?"

Hobbs licked his lips. He choked, then whispered
hoarsely: "Nobody . . . but there's . . . there's a back
stairs."

Sabre wheeled and walked back in quick strides,
thumbing shells into his gun. The office door was
open, and Prince McCarran looked up as he framed
himself in the door.

He was writing, and the desk was rumpled with
papers, the desk of a busy man. Nearby was a bottle
and a full glass.

McCarran lay down his pen. "So? You beat him? I
thought you might."

"Did you?" Sabre's gaze was cold. If this man had
been running, as he must have run, he gave no evi-
dence of it now. "You should hire them faster,
Prince."

"Well"—McCarran shrugged—"he was fast enough
until now. But this wasn't my job, anyway. He was
workin' for Reed."

Sabre took a step inside the door, away from the wall, keeping his hands free. His eyes were on those of Prince McCarran, and Prince watched him, alert, interested.

"That won't ride with me," Matt said. "Reed's a stooge, a perfect stooge. He'll be lucky if he comes back alive from this trip. A lot of that posse you sent out won't come back, either."

McCarran's eyelids tightened at the mention of the posse. "Forget it." He waved his hand. "Sit down and have a drink. After all, we're not fools, Sabre. We're grown men, and we can talk. I never liked killing, anyway."

"Unless you do it or have it done." Sabre's hands remained where they were. "What's the matter, Prince? Yellow? Afraid to do your own killin'?"

McCarran's face was still, and his eyes were wide now. "You shouldn't have said that. You shouldn't have called me yellow."

"Then get on your feet. I hate to shoot a sittin' man."

"Have a drink and let's talk."

"Sure." Sabre was elaborately casual. "You have one, too." He reached his hand for the glass that had already been poured, but McCarran's eyes were steady. Sabre switched his hand and grasped the other glass, and then, like a striking snake, Prince McCarran grasped his right hand and jerked him forward, off balance.

At the same time, McCarran's left flashed back to

174

the holster high on his left side, butt forward, and the gun jerked up and free. Matt Sabre, instead of trying to jerk his right hand free, let his weight go forward, following and hurling himself against McCarran. The chair went over with a *crash*, and Prince tried to straighten, but Matt was riding him back. He crashed into the wall, and Sabre broke free.

Prince swung his gun up, and Sabre's left palm slapped down, knocking the gun aside and gripping the hand across the thumb. His right hand came up under the gun barrel, twisting it back over and out of McCarran's hands. Then he shoved him back and dropped the gun, slapping him across the mouth with his open palm.

It was a free swing, and it *cracked* like a pistol shot. McCarran's face went white from the blow, and he rushed, swinging, but Sabre brought up his knee in the charging man's groin. Then he smashed him in the face with his elbow, pushing him over and back. McCarran dived past him, blood streaming from his crushed nose, and grabbed wildly at the papers. His hand came up with a bulldog .41.

Matt saw the hand shoot for the papers, and, even as the .41 appeared, his own gun was lifting. He fired first, three times, at a range of four feet.

Prince McCarran stiffened, lifted to his tiptoes, then plunged over on his face, and lay still among the litter of papers and broken glass.

Sabre swayed drunkenly. He recalled what Sikes had said about the desk. He caught the edge and jerked it aside, swinging the desk away from the wall. Behind it was a small panel with a knob. It was locked, but a bullet smashed the lock. He jerked it open. A thick wad of bills, a small sack of gold coins, a sheaf of papers.

A glance sufficed. These were the papers Simpson had mentioned. The thick parchment of the original grant, the information on the conflicting Sonoma grant, and then. . . . He glanced swiftly through them, then, at a pound of horses' hoofs, he stuffed them inside his shirt. He stopped, stared. His shirt was soaked with blood.

Fumbling, he got the papers into his pocket, then stared down at himself. Sikes had hit him. Funny, he had never felt it. Only a shock, a numbness. Now Reed was coming back.

Catching up a sawed-off express shotgun, he started for the door, weaving like a drunken man. He never even got to the door.

The sound of galloping horses was all he could hear— galloping horses, and then a faint smell of something that reminded him of a time he had been wounded in North Africa. His eyes flickered open, and the first thing he saw was a room's wall with the picture of a man with muttonchop whiskers and spectacles.

He turned his head and saw Jenny Curtin watching him. "So? You've decided to wake up. You're getting lazy, Matt. Mister Sabre. On the ranch you always were the first one up."

He stared at her. She had never looked half so charming, and that was bad. It was bad because it was time to be out of here and on a horse.

"How long have I been here?"

"Only about a day and a half. You lost a lot of blood."

"What happened at the ranch? Did Keys get there in time?"

"Yes, and I stayed. The others left right away."

"You stayed?"

"The others," she said quietly, "went down the road about two miles. There were Camp Gordon, Tom Judson, Pepito, and Keys. And Rado, of course. They went down the road while I stood out in the ranch yard and let them see me. The boys ambushed them."

"Was it much of a fight?"

"None at all. The surprise was so great that they broke and ran. Only three weren't able, and four were badly wounded."

"You found the papers? Including the one about McCarran sending the five thousand in marked bills to El Paso?"

"Yes," she said simply. "We found that. He planned on having Billy arrested and charged with theft. He planned that, and then, if he got killed, so much the better. It was only you he didn't count on."

"No." Matt Sabre stared at his hands, strangely white now. "He didn't count on me."

So it was all over now. She had her ranch, she was

a free woman, and people would leave her alone. There was only one thing left. He had to tell her. To tell her that he was the one who had killed her husband.

He turned his head on the pillow. "One thing more," he began. "I. . . ."

"Not now. You need rest."

"Wait. I have to tell you this. It's about . . . about Billy."

"You mean that you . . . you were the one who . . . ?"

"Yes, I. . . ." He hesitated, reluctant at last to say it.

"I know. I know you did, Matt. I've known from the beginning, even without all the things you said."

"I talked when I was delirious?"

"A little. But I knew, Matt. Call it intuition, anything you like, but I knew. You see, you told me how his eyes were when he was drawing his gun. Who could have known that but the man who shot him?"

"I see." His face was white. "Then I'd better rest. I've got some traveling to do."

She was standing beside him. "Traveling? Do you have to go on, Matt? From all you said last night, I thought . . . I thought"— her face flushed—"maybe you . . . didn't want to travel any more. Stay with us, Matt, if you want to. We would like to have you, and Billy's been asking for you. He wants to know where his spurs are."

After a while, he admitted carefully: "Well, I guess I should stay and see that he gets them. A fellow should always make good on his promises to kids, I reckon."

"You'll stay, then? You won't leave?"

Matt stared up at her. "I reckon," he said quietly, "I'll never leave unless you send me away."

She smiled and touched his hair. "Then you'll be here a long time, Mathurin Sabre . . . a very long time."

War Party

We buried Pa on a side hill out west of camp, buried him high up so his ghost could look down the trail he'd planned to travel.

We piled the grave high with rocks because of the coyotes, and we dug the grave deep, and some of it I dug myself, and Mr. Sampson helped, and some others.

Folks in the wagon train figured Ma would turn back, but they hadn't known Ma so long as I had. Once she set her mind to something, she wasn't about to quit.

She was a young woman and pretty, but there was strength in her. She was a lone woman with two children, but she was of no mind to turn back. She'd come through the Little Crow massacre in Minnesota and she knew what trouble was. Yet it was like her that she put it up to me.

"Bud," she said, when we were alone, "we can turn back, but we've nobody there who cares about us, and it's of you and Jeanie that I'm thinking. If we go West, you will have to be the man of the house, and you'll have to work hard to make up for Pa."

"We'll go West," I said. A boy those days took it for granted that he had work to do, and the men couldn't do it all. No boy ever thought of himself as only twelve or thirteen or whatever he was, being anxious to prove himself and take a man's place and responsibilities.

Ryerson and his wife were going back. She was a complaining woman and he was a man who was always ailing when there was work to be done. Four or five wagons were turning back, folks with their tails betwixt their legs running for the shelter of towns where their own littleness wouldn't stand out so plain.

When a body crossed the Mississippi and left the settlements behind, something happened to him. The world seemed to bust wide open, and suddenly the horizons spread out and a man wasn't cramped any more. The pinched-up villages and the narrowness of towns, all that was gone. The horizons simply exploded and rolled back into the enormous distance, with nothing around but prairie and sky.

Some folks couldn't stand it. They'd cringe into themselves and start hunting excuses to go back where they came from. This was a big country needing big men and women to live in it, and there was no place out here for the frightened or the mean.

The prairie and sky had a way of trimming folks down to size, or changing them to giants to whom nothing seemed impossible. Men who had cut a wide swath back in the States found themselves nothing out here. They were folks who were used to doing a lot of talking who suddenly found that no one was listening any more, and things that seemed mighty important back home, like family and money, they amounted to nothing alongside character and courage.

There was John Sampson from our town. He was a man used to being told to do things, used to looking up to wealth and power, but when he crossed the Mississippi, he began to lift his head and look around. He squared his shoulders, put more crack to his whip, and began to make his own tracks in the land.

Pa was always strong, an independent man given to reading at night from one of the four or five books we had, to speaking up on matters of principle, and to straight shooting with a rifle. Pa had fought the Comanches and lived with the Sioux, but he wasn't strong enough to last more than two days with a Kiowa arrow through his lung. But he died knowing Ma had stood by the rear wheel and shot the Kiowa whose arrow was in him.

Right then I knew that neither Indians nor country was going to get the better of Ma. Shooting that Kiowa was the first time Ma had shot anything but some chicken-killing varmint—which she'd done time to time when Pa was away from home.

Only Ma wouldn't let Jeanie and me call it home. "We came here from Illinois," she said, "but we're going home now."

"But Ma," I protested, "I thought home was where we came from?"

"Home is where we're going now," Ma said, "and we'll know it when we find it. Now that Pa is gone, we'll have to build that home ourselves."

She had a way of saying *home* so it sounded like a

rare and wonderful place and kept Jeanie and me looking always at the horizon, just knowing it was over there, waiting for us to see it. She had given us the dream, and even Jeanie, who was only six, she had it, too.

She might tell us that home was where we were going, but I knew home was where Ma was, a warm and friendly place with biscuits on the table and fresh-made butter. We wouldn't have a real home until Ma was there and we had a fire going. Only I'd build the fire.

Mr. Buchanan, who was captain of the wagon train, came to us with Tryon Burt, who was guide. "We'll help you," Mr. Buchanan said. "I know you'll be wanting to go back, and. . . ."

"But we are not going back." Ma smiled at them. "And don't be afraid we'll be a burden. I know you have troubles of your own, and we will manage very well."

Mr. Buchanan looked uncomfortable, like he was trying to think of the right thing to say. "Now, see here," he protested, "we started this trip with a rule. There has to be a man with every wagon."

Ma put her hand on my shoulder. "I have my man. Bud is almost thirteen and accepts responsibility. I could ask for no better man."

Ryerson came up. He was thin, stooped in the shoulder, and, whenever he looked at Ma, there was a greasy look to his eyes that I didn't like. He was a man who looked dirty even when he'd just washed in

183

the creek. "You come along with me, ma'am," he said. "I'll take good care of you."

"Mister Ryerson"—Ma looked him right in the eye—"you have a wife who can use better care than she's getting, and I have my son."

"He's nothin' but a boy."

"You are turning back, are you not? My son is going on. I believe that should indicate who is more the man. It is neither size nor age that makes a man, Mister Ryerson, but something he has inside. My son has it."

Ryerson might have said something unpleasant only Tryon Burt was standing there wishing he would, so he just looked ugly and hustled off.

"I'd like to say you could come," Mr. Buchanan said, "but the boy couldn't stand up to a man's work."

Ma smiled at him, chin up, the way she had. "I do not believe in gambling, Mister Buchanan, but I'll wager a good Ballard rifle there isn't a man in camp who could follow a child all day, running when it runs, squatting when it squats, bending when it bends, and wrestling when it wrestles, and not be played out long before the child is."

"You may be right, ma'am, but a rule is a rule."

"We are in Indian country, Mister Buchanan. If you are killed a week from now, I suppose your wife must return to the States?"

"That's different! Nobody could turn back from there!"

"Then," Ma said sweetly, "it seems a rule is only a rule within certain limits, and, if I recall correctly, no such limit was designated in the articles of travel. Whatever limits there were, Mister Buchanan, must have been passed sometime before the Indian attack that killed my husband."

"I can drive the wagon, and so can Ma," I said. "For the past two days I've been driving, and nobody said anything until Pa died."

Mr. Buchanan didn't know what to say, but a body could see he didn't like it. Nor did he like a woman who talked up to him the way Ma did.

Tryon Burt spoke up. "Let the boy drive. I've watched this youngster, and he'll do. He has better judgment than most men in the outfit, and he stands up to his work. If need be, I'll help."

Mr. Buchanan turned around and walked off with his back stiff the way it is when he's mad. Ma looked at Burt, and she said: "Thank you, Mister Burt. That was nice of you."

Try Burt, he got all red around the gills and took off like somebody had put a burr under his saddle.

Come morning, our wagon was the second one ready to take its place in line, with both horses saddled and tied behind the wagon, and me standing beside the off ox.

Any direction a man wanted to look, there was nothing but grass and sky, only sometimes there'd be a buffalo wallow or a gopher hole. We made eleven miles the first day after Pa was buried, sixteen the next, then nineteen, thirteen, and twenty-one. At no time did the country change. On the sixth day after Pa died I killed a buffalo.

It was a young bull, but a big one, and I spotted him coming up out of a draw and was off my horse and bellied down in the grass before Try Burt realized there was game in sight. That bull came up from the draw and stopped there, staring at the wagon train, which was a half mile off. Setting a sight behind his left shoulder, I took a long breath, took in the trigger slack, then squeezed off my shot so gentle-like the gun jumped in my hands before I was ready for it.

The bull took a step back like something had surprised him, and I jacked another shell into the chamber and was sighting on him again when he went down on his knees, and rolled over on his side.

"You got him, Bud!" Burt was more excited than I. "That was shootin'!"

Try got down and showed me how to skin the bull, and lent me a hand. Then we cut out a lot of fresh meat and toted it back to the wagons.

Ma was at the fire when we came up, a wisp of brown hair alongside her cheek and her face flushed from the heat of the fire, looking as pretty as a bay pony.

"Bud killed his first buffalo," Burt told her, looking at Ma like he could eat her with a spoon.

"Why, Bud! That's wonderful!" Her eyes started to

dance with a kind of mischief in them, and she said: "Bud, why don't you take a piece of that meat along to Mister Buchanan and the others?"

With Burt to help, we cut the meat into eighteen pieces and distributed it around the wagons. It wasn't much, but it was the first fresh meat in a couple of weeks.

John Sampson squeezed my shoulder and said: "Seems to me you and your Ma are folks to travel with. This outfit needs some hunters."

Each night I staked out that buffalo hide, and each day I worked at curing it before rolling it up to pack on the wagon. Believe you me, I was some proud of that buffalo hide. Biggest thing I'd shot until then was a cottontail rabbit back in Illinois, where we lived when I was born. Try Burt told folks about that shot. "Two hundred yards," he'd say, "right through the heart."

Only it wasn't more than 150 yards the way I figured, and Pa used to make me pace off distances, so I'd learn to judge right. But I was nobody to argue with Try Burt telling a story—besides, 200 yards makes an awful lot better sound than 150.

After supper, the menfolks would gather to talk plans. The season was late, and we weren't making the time we ought if we hoped to beat the snow through the passes of the Sierras. When they talked, I was there because I was the man of my wagon, but nobody paid me no mind. Mr. Buchanan, he acted like he didn't see me, but John Sampson would and Try Burt always smiled at me.

Several spoke up for turning back, but Mr. Buchanan said he knew of an outfit that made it through later than this. One thing was sure. Our wagon wasn't turning back. Like Ma said, home was somewhere ahead of us, and back in the States we'd have no money and nobody to turn to, nor any relatives, anywhere. It was the three of us.

"We're going on," I said at one of these talks. "We don't figure to turn back for anything."

Webb gave me a glance full of contempt. "You'll go where the rest of us go. You an' your Ma would play hob gettin' by on your own."

Next day it rained, dawn to dark it fairly poured, and we were lucky to make six miles. Day after that, with the wagon wheels sinking into the prairie and the rain still falling, we camped just two miles from where we started in the morning.

Nobody talked much around the fires, and what was said was apt to be short and irritable. Most of these folks had put all they owned into the outfits they had, and, if they turned back now, they'd have nothing to live on and nothing left to make a fresh start. Except a few like Mr. Buchanan, who was well off.

"It doesn't have to be California," Ma said once. "What most of us want is land, not gold."

"This here is Indian country," John Sampson said, "and a sight too open for me. I'd like a valley in the hills, with running water close by."

"There will be valleys and meadows," Ma replied,

stirring the stew she was making, "and tall trees near running streams, and tall grass growing in the meadows, and there will be game in the forest and on the grassy plains, and places for homes."

"And where will we find all that?" Webb's tone was slighting.

"West," Ma said, "over against the mountains."

"I suppose you've been there?" Webb scoffed.

"No, Mister Webb, I haven't been there, but I've been told of it. The land is there, and we will have some of it, my children and I, and we will stay through the winter, and in the spring we will plant our crops."

"Easy to say."

"This is Sioux country to the north," Burt said. "We'll be lucky to get through without a fight. There was a war party of thirty or thirty-five passed this way a couple of days ago."

"Sioux?"

"Uhn-huh . . . no women or children along, and I found some war paint rubbed off on the brush."

"Maybe," Mr. Buchanan suggested, "we'd better turn south a mite."

"It is late in the season," Ma replied, "and the straightest way is the best way now."

"No use to worry," White interrupted. "Those Indians went on by. They won't likely know we're around."

"They were riding southeast," Ma said, "and their home is in the north, so when they return, they'll be riding northwest. There is no way they can miss our trail."

"Then we'd best turn back," White said.

"Don't look like we'd make it this year, anyway," a woman said. "The season is late."

That started the argument, and some were for turning back and some wanted to push on, and finally White said we should push on, but travel fast.

"Fast?" Webb asked disparagingly. "An Indian can ride in one day the distance we'd travel in four."

That started the wrangling again and Ma continued with her cooking. Sitting there watching her, I figured I never did see anybody so graceful or quick on her feet as Ma, and, when we used to walk in the woods back home, I never knew her to stumble or step on a fallen twig or branch.

The group broke up and returned to their own fires with nothing settled, only there at the end Mr. Buchanan looked to Burt. "Do you know the Sioux?"

"Only the Utes and Shoshones, and I spent a winter on the Snake with the Nez Percés one time. But I've had no truck with the Sioux. Only they tell me they're bad medicine. Fightin' men from 'way back and they don't cotton to white folks in their country. If we run into Sioux, we're in trouble."

After Mr. Buchanan had gone, Tryon Burt accepted a plate and cup from Ma and settled down to eating. After a while he looked up at her and said: "Beggin' your pardon, ma'am, but it struck me you knew a sight about trackin' for an Eastern woman. You'd spotted those Sioux your own self, an' you figured it right that they'd pick up our trail on the way back."

She smiled at him. "It was simply an observation, Mister Burt. I would believe anyone would notice it. I simply put it into words."

Burt went on eating, but he was mighty thoughtful, and it didn't seem to me he was satisfied with Ma's answer.

Ma said finally: "It seems to be raining west of here. Isn't it likely to be snowing in the mountains?"

Burt looked up uneasily. "Not necessarily so, ma'am. It could be raining here and not snowing there, but I'd say there was a chance of snow." He got up and came around the fire to the coffee pot. "What are you gettin' at, ma'am?"

"Some of them are ready to turn back or change their plans. What will you do then?"

He frowned, placing his cup on the grass and starting to fill his pipe. "No idea . . . might head south for Santa Fé. Why do you ask?"

"Because we're going on," Ma said. "We're going to the mountains, and I am hoping some of the others decide to come with us."

"You'd go alone?" He was amazed.

"If necessary."

We started on at daybreak, but folks were more scary than before, and they kept looking at the great distances stretching away on either side, and muttering. There was an autumn coolness in the air, and we

191

were still short of South Pass by several days with the memory of the Donner party being talked up around us.

There was another kind of talk in the wagons, and some of it I heard. The nightly gatherings around Ma's fire had started talk, and some of it pointed to Tryon Burt, and some were saying other things.

We made seventeen miles that day, and at night Mr. Buchanan didn't come to our fire. When White stopped by, his wife came and got him. Ma looked at her and smiled, and Mrs. White sniffed and went away beside her husband.

"Mister Burt"—Ma wasn't one to beat around a bush—"is there talk about me?"

Try Burt got red around the ears and he opened his mouth, but couldn't find the words he wanted. "Maybe . . . well, maybe I shouldn't eat here all the time. Only . . . well, ma'am, you're the best cook in camp."

Ma smiled at him. "I hope that isn't the only reason you come to see us, Mister Burt."

He got redder than ever then and gulped his coffee and took off in a hurry.

Time to time the men had stopped by to help a little, but next morning nobody came by. We got lined out about as soon as ever, and Ma said to me as we sat on the wagon seat: "Pay no attention, Bud. You've no call to take up anything if you don't notice it. There will always be folks who will talk, and the better you do in the world, the more bad things they

192

will say of you. Back there in the settlement you remember how the dogs used to run out and bark at our wagons?"

"Yes, Ma."

"Did the wagons stop?"

"No, Ma."

"Remember that, Son. The dogs bark, but the wagons go on their way, and, if you're going some place, you haven't time to bother with barking dogs."

We made eighteen miles that day, and the grass was better, but there was a rumble of distant thunder, whimpering and muttering off in the cañons, promising rain.

Webb stopped by, dropped an armful of wood beside the fire, then started off.

"Thank you, Mister Webb," Ma said, "but aren't you afraid you'll be talked about?"

He looked angry and started to reply something angry, and then he grinned and said: "I reckon I'd be flattered, Missus Miles."

Ma said: "No matter what is decided by the rest of them, Mister Webb, we are going on, but there is no need to go to California for what we want."

Webb took out his pipe and tamped it. He had a dark, devil's face on him with eyebrows like you see on pictures of the devil. I was afraid of Mr. Webb.

"We want land," Ma said, "and there is land around us. In the mountains ahead there will be streams and forests, there will be fish and game, logs for houses and meadows for grazing."

193

Mr. Buchanan had joined us. "That's fool talk," he declared. "What could anyone do in these hills? You'd be cut off from the world. Left out of it."

"A man wouldn't be so crowded as in California," John Sampson remarked. "I've seen so many go that I've been wondering what they all do there."

"For a woman," Webb replied, ignoring the others, "you've a head on you, ma'am."

"What about the Sioux?" Mr. Buchanan asked dryly.

"We'd not be encroaching on their land. They live to the north," Ma said. She gestured toward the mountains. "There is land to be had just a few days farther on, and that is where our wagon will stop."

A few days! Everybody looked at everybody else. Not months, but days only. Those who stopped then would have enough of their supplies left to help them through the winter, and with what game they could kill—and time for cutting wood and even building cabins before the cold set in.

Oh, there was an argument, such argument as you've never heard, and the upshot of it was that all agreed it was fool talk and the thing to do was keep going. And there was talk I overheard about Ma being no better than she should be, and why was that guide always hanging around her? And all those men? No decent woman—I hurried away.

At break of day our wagons rolled down a long valley with a small stream alongside the trail, and the

Indians came over the ridge to the south of us and started our way—tall, fine-looking men with feathers in their hair.

There was barely time for a circle, but I was riding off in front with Tryon Burt, and he said: "A man can always try to talk first, and Injuns like a palaver. You get back to the wagons."

Only I rode along beside him, my rifle over my saddle and ready to hand. My mouth was dry and my heart was beating so's I thought Try could hear it, I was that scared. But behind us the wagons were making their circle, and every second was important.

Their chief was a big man with splendid muscles, and there was a scalp not many days old hanging from his lance. It looked like Ryerson's hair, but Ryerson's wagons should have been miles away to the east by now.

Burt tried them in Shoshone, but it was the language of their enemies and they merely stared at him, understanding well enough, but of no mind to talk. One young buck kept staring at Burt with a taunt in his eye, daring Burt to make a move; then suddenly the chief spoke, and they all turned their eyes toward the wagons.

There was a rider coming, and it was a woman. It was Ma.

She rode right up beside us, and, when she drew up, she started to talk, and she was speaking their language. She was talking Sioux. We both knew what it was because those Indians sat up and paid attention. Suddenly she directed a question at the chief.

"Red Horse," he said in English.

Ma shifted to English. "My husband was blood brother to Gall, the greatest warrior of the Sioux nation. It was my husband who found Gall dying in the brush with a bayonet wound in his chest, who took Gall to his home and treated the wound until it was well."

"Your husband was a medicine man?" Red Horse asked.

"My husband was a warrior," Ma replied proudly, "but he made war only against strong men, not women or children or the wounded." She put her hand on my shoulder. "This is my son. As my husband was blood brother to Gall, his son is by blood brotherhood the son of Gall, also."

Red Horse stared at Ma for a long time, and I was getting even more scared. I could feel a drop of sweat start at my collar and crawl slowly down my spine. Red Horse looked at me. "Is this one a fit son for Gall?"

"He is a fit son. He has killed his first buffalo."

Red Horse turned his mount and spoke to the others. One of the young braves shouted angrily at him, and Red Horse replied sharply. Reluctantly the warriors trailed off after their chief.

"Ma'am," Burt said, "you just about saved our bacon. They were just spoilin' for a fight."

"We should be moving," Ma said.

Mr. Buchanan was waiting for us. "What happened out there? I tried to keep her back, but she's a difficult woman."

"She's worth any three men in the outfit," Burt replied.

That day we made eighteen miles, and by the time the wagons circled there was talk. The fact that Ma had saved them was less important now than other things. It didn't seem right that a decent woman could talk Sioux or mix in the affairs of men.

Nobody came to our fire, but while picketing the saddle horses, I heard someone say: "Must be part Injun. Else why would they pay attention to a woman?"

"Maybe she's part Injun and leadin' us into a trap."

"Hadn't been for her," Burt said, "you'd all be dead now."

"How do you know what she said to 'em? Who savvies that lingo?"

"I never did trust that woman," Mrs. White said. "Too high and mighty. Nor that husband of hers, either, comes to that. Kept to himself too much."

The air was cool after a brief shower when we started in the morning, and no Indians in sight. All day long we moved over grass made fresh by new rain, and all the ridges were pine-clad now, and the growth along the streams heavier. Short of sundown I killed an antelope with a running shot, dropped him mighty neat—and looked up to see an Indian watching from a hill. At the distance I couldn't tell, but it could have been Red Horse.

Time to time I'd passed along the train, but nobody waved or said anything. Webb watched me go by, his face stolid as one of the Sioux, yet I could see there was a deal of talk going on.

"Why are they mad at us?" I asked Burt.

"Folks hate something they don't understand, or anything seems different. Your ma goes her own way, speaks her mind, and of an evening she doesn't set by and gossip."

He topped out on a rise and drew up to study the country, and me beside him. "You got to figure most of these folks come from small towns where they never knew much aside from their families, their gossip, and their church. It doesn't seem right to them that a decent woman would find time to learn Sioux."

Burt studied the country. "Time was, any stranger was an enemy, and, if anybody came around who wasn't one of yours, you killed him. I've seen wolves jump on a wolf that was white or different somehow . . . seems like folks and animals fear anything that's unusual."

We circled, and I staked out my horses and took the oxen to the herd. By the time Ma had her grub box lid down, I was fixing at a fire when here come Mr. Buchanan, Mr. and Mrs. White, and some other folks, including that Webb.

"Ma'am"—Mr. Buchanan was mighty abrupt—

"we figure we ought to know what you said to those Sioux. We want to know why they turned off just because you went out there."

"Does it matter?"

Mr. Buchanan's face stiffened up. "We think it does. There's some think you might be an Indian your own self."

"And if I am?" Ma was amused. "Just what is it you have in mind, Mister Buchanan?"

"We don't want no Injuns in this outfit!" Mr. White shouted.

"How does it come you can talk that language?" Mrs. White demanded. "Even Tryon Burt can't talk it."

"I figure maybe you want us to keep goin' because there's a trap up ahead," White declared.

I never realized folks could be so mean, but there they were facing Ma like they hated her, like those witch hunters Ma told me about back in Salem. It didn't seem right that Ma, who they didn't like, had saved them from an Indian attack, and the fact that she talked Sioux like any Indian bothered them.

"As it happens," Ma said, "I am not an Indian, although I should not be ashamed of it if I were. They have many admirable qualities. However, you need worry yourselves no longer, as we part company in the morning. I have no desire to travel further with you . . . *gentlemen*."

Mr. Buchanan's face got all angry, and he started up to say something mean. Nobody was about to

199

speak roughly to Ma with me standing by, so I just picked up that old rifle and jacked a shell into the chamber. "Mister Buchanan, this here's my ma, and she's a lady, so you just be careful what words you use."

"Put down that rifle, you young fool!" he shouted at me.

"Mister Buchanan, I may be little and may be a fool, but this here rifle doesn't care who pulls its trigger."

He looked like he was going to have a stroke, but he just turned sharply around and walked away, all stiff in the back.

"Ma'am," Webb said, "you've no cause to like me much, but you've shown more brains than that passel o' fools. If you'll be so kind, me and my boy would like to trail along with you."

"I like a man who speaks his mind, Mister Webb. I would consider it an honor to have your company."

Tryon Burt looked quizzically at Ma. "Why, now, seems to me this is a time for a man to make up his mind, and I'd like to be included along with Webb."

"Mister Burt," Ma said, "for your own information, I grew up among Sioux children in Minnesota. They were my playmates."

Come daylight our wagon pulled off to one side, pointing northwest at the mountains, and Mr. Buchanan led off to the west. Webb followed Ma's wagon, and I sat watching Mr. Buchanan's eyes get angrier as John Sampson, Neely Stuart, the two

Shafter wagons, and Tom Croft all fell in behind us.

Tryon Burt had been talking to Mr. Buchanan, but he left off and trotted his horse over to where I sat my horse. Mr. Buchanan looked mighty sullen when he saw half his wagon train gone and with it a lot of his importance as captain.

Two days and nearly forty miles farther and we topped out on a rise and paused to let the oxen take a blow. A long valley lay across our route, with tall grass wet with rain, and a flat bench on the mountainside seen through a gray veil of a light shower falling. There was that bench, with the white trunks of aspen on the mountainside beyond it looking like ranks of slim soldiers guarding the bench against the storms.

"Ma," I said.

"All right, Bud," she said quietly, "we've come home."

And I started up the oxen and drove down into the valley where I was to become a man.

Law of the Desert

I

Shad Marone crawled out of the water, swearing, and slid into the mesquite. Suddenly, for the first time since the chase began, he was mad. He was mad clear through. "The hell with it!" He got to his feet, his eyes blazing. "I've run far enough! If they cross Black River, they're askin' for it!"

For three days he had been on the dodge, using every stratagem known to men of the desert, but they clung to him like leeches. That was what came of killing a sheriff's brother, and the fact that he killed in self-defense wasn't going to help a bit. Especially when the killer was Shad Marone.

That was what you could expect when you were the last man of the losing side in a cattle war. All his friends were gone now but Madge.

The best people of Puerto de Luna hadn't been the toughest in this scrap, and they had lost. And Shad Marone, who had been one of the toughest, had lost with them. His guns hadn't been enough to outweigh those of the other faction.

Of course, he admitted to himself, those on his side hadn't been angels. He'd branded a few head of calves himself from time to time, and, when cash was short, he had often run a few steers over the border. But hadn't they all?

Truman and Dykes had been good men, but Dykes had been killed at the start, and Truman had fought like a gentleman, and that wasn't any way to win in the Black River country.

Since then, there had been few peaceful days for Shad Marone.

After they'd elected Clyde Bowman sheriff, he knew they were out to get him. Bowman hated him, and Bowman had been one of the worst of them in the cattle war.

The trouble was, Shad was a gunfighter, and they all knew it. Bowman was fast with a gun and in a fight could hold his own. Also, he was smart enough to leave Shad Marone strictly alone. So they just waited, watched, and planned.

Shad had taken their dislike as a matter of course. It took tough men to settle a tough country, and, if they started shooting, somebody got hurt. Well, he wasn't getting hurt. There had been too much shooting to suit him.

He had wanted to leave Puerto de Luna, but Madge was still living on the old place, and he didn't want to leave her there alone. So he had stayed on, knowing it couldn't last.

Then Jud Bowman rode into town. Shad was thoughtful when he heard that. Jud was notoriously quarrelsome and was said to have twelve notches on his gun. Shad had a feeling that Jud hadn't come to Puerto de Luna by accident.

Jud hadn't been in town two days before the

grapevine had the story that, if Clyde and Lopez were afraid to run Marone out of town, he wasn't.

Jud Bowman might have done it, too, if it hadn't been for Tips. Tips Hogan had been tending bar in Puerto de Luna for a long time. He'd come over the trail as wagon boss for Shad's old man, something everyone had forgotten but Shad and Tips himself.

Tips saw the gun in Bowman's lap, and he gave Marone a warning. It was just a word, through unmoving lips, while he mopped the bar.

After a moment, Shad turned, his glass in his left hand, and he saw the way Bowman was sitting and how the table top would conceal a gun in his lap. Even then, when he knew they had set things up to kill him, he hadn't wanted trouble. He decided to get out while the getting was good. Then he saw Slade near the door and Henderson across the room.

He was boxed. They weren't gambling this time. Tips Hogan knew what was likely to happen, and he was working his way down the bar.

Marone took it easy. He knew it was coming, and it wasn't a new thing. That was his biggest advantage, he thought. He had been in more fights than any of them. He didn't want any more trouble, but if he got out of this, it would be right behind a six-gun. The back door was barred and the window closed.

Jud Bowman looked up suddenly. He had a great shock of blond, coarse hair, and under bushy brows his eyes glinted. "What's this about you threatenin' to kill me, Marone?"

So that was their excuse. He had not threatened Bowman, scarcely knew him, in fact, but this was the way to put him in the wrong, to give them the plea of self-defense.

He let his eyes turn to Bowman, saw the tension in the man's face. A denial, and there would be shooting. Jud's right-hand fingertips rested on the table's edge. He had only to drop a hand and fire.

"Huh?" Shad said stupidly, as though startled from a daydream. He took a step toward the table, his face puzzled. "Wha'd you say? I didn't get it."

They had planned it all very carefully. Marone would deny, Bowman would claim he'd been called a liar, there would be a killing. They were tense, all three of them set to draw.

"Huh?" Shad repeated blankly.

They were caught flat-footed. After all, you couldn't shoot a man in cold blood. You couldn't shoot a man who was half asleep. Most of the men in the saloon were against Marone, but they would never stand for murder.

They were poised for action, and nothing happened. Shad blinked at them. "Sorry," he said, "I must've been dreamin'. I didn't hear you."

Bowman glanced around uncertainly, wetting his lips with his tongue. "I said I heard you threatened to kill me," he repeated. It sounded lame, and he knew it, but Shad's response had been unexpected. What happened then was even more unexpected.

Marone's left hand shot out, and, before anyone

could move, the table was spun from in front of Bowman. Everyone saw the naked gun lying in his lap.

Every man in the saloon knew that Jud Bowman, for all his reputation, had been afraid to shoot it out with an even break. It would have been murder.

Taken by surprise, Bowman blinked foolishly. Then his wits came back. Blood rushed to his face. He grabbed the gun. "Why, you . . . !"

Then Shad Marone shot him. Shad shot him through the belly, and, before the other two could act, he wheeled, not toward the door, but to the closed window. He battered it with his shoulder and went right on through. Outside, he hit the ground on his hands, but came up in a lunging run. Then he was in the saddle and on his way.

There were men in the saloon who would tell the truth—two at least, although neither had much use for him. But Marone knew that with Clyde Bowman as sheriff he would never be brought to trial. He would be killed "evading arrest."

For three days he fled, and during that time they were never more than an hour behind him. Then, at Forked Tree, they closed in. He got away, but they clipped his horse. The roan stayed on his feet, giving all he had, as horses always had given for Shad Marone, and then died on the riverbank, still trying with his last breath.

Marone took time to cache his saddle and bridle, then started on afoot. He made the river, and they thought that would stop him, for he couldn't swim a stroke. But he found a drift log, and with his guns riding high he shoved off. Using the current and his own kicking, he got to the other bank, considerably downstream.

The thing that bothered him was the way they clung to his trail. Bowman wasn't the man to follow as little trail as he left. Yet the man hung to him like an Apache.

Apache!

Why hadn't he thought of that? It would be Lopez following that trail, not Bowman. Bowman was a bulldog, but Lopez was wily as a fox and blood-thirsty as a weasel.

Shad got to his feet and shook the water from him like a dog. He was a big, raw-boned, sun-browned man. His shirt was half torn away, and a bandoleer of cartridges was slung across his shoulder and chest. His six-gun was on his hip, his rifle in his hand.

He poured the water out of his boots. Well, he was through playing now. If they wanted a trail, he'd see that they got one.

Lopez was the one who worried him. He could shake the others, but Lopez was one of the men who had built this country. He was ugly, he killed freely and often, he was absolutely ruthless, but he had nerve. You had to hand it to him. The man wasn't honest, and he was too quick to kill, but it had taken men like him to tame this wild, lonely land. It was a land that didn't tame easy.

Well, what they'd get now would be death for them all. Even Lopez. This was something he'd been saving.

Grimly he turned up the steep, little-used path from the river. They thought they had him at the river. And they would think they had him again at the lava beds.

Waterless, treeless, and desolate, the lava beds were believed to harbor no life of any kind. Only sand and great, jagged rocks—rocks shaped like flame—grotesque, barren, awful. More than seventy miles long, never less than thirty miles wide, so rough a pair of shoes wouldn't last five miles and footing next to impossible for horses.

On the edge of the lava, Shad Marone sat down and pulled off his boots. Tying their strings, he hung them to his belt. Then he pulled out a pair of moccasins he always carried and slipped them on. Pliable and easy on his feet, they would give to the rough rock and would last many times as long in this terrain as boots. He got up and walked into the lava beds.

The bare lava caught the fierce heat and threw it back in his face. A trickle of sweat started down his cheek. He knew the desert, knew how to live in the heat, and he did not try to hurry. That would be fatal. Far ahead of him was a massive tower of rock jutting up like a church steeple from a tiny village. He headed that way, walking steadily. He made no attempt to cover his trail, no attempt to lose his pursuers. He knew where he was going.

An hour passed, and then another. It was slow

going. The rock tower had come abreast of him, and then fallen behind. Once he saw the trail of some tiny creature, perhaps a horned frog.

Once, when he climbed a steep declivity, he glanced back. They were still coming. They hadn't quit.

Lopez—that was like Lopez. He wouldn't quit. Shad smiled then, but his eyes were without humor. All right, they wanted to kill him badly enough to try the lava beds. They would have to learn the hard way—learn when they could never profit from the lesson.

He kept working north, using the shade carefully. There was little of it, only here and there in the lee of a rock. But each time he stopped, he cooled off a little. So far he hadn't taken a drink.

After the third hour, he washed his lips and rinsed his mouth. Twice, after that, he took only a spoonful of water and rinsed his mouth before swallowing.

Occasionally he stopped and looked around to get his bearings. He smiled grimly when he thought of Bowman. The sheriff was a heavy man. Davis would be there, too. Lopez was lean and wiry. He would last. He would be hard to kill.

By his last count, there were eight left. Four had turned back at the lava beds. He gained a little.

At 3:00 in the afternoon, he finally stopped. It was a nice piece of shade and would grow better as the hours went on. The ground was low, and in one corner there was a pocket. He dug with his hands until the ground became damp. Then he lay back on the sand and went to sleep.

He wasn't worried. Too many years he had been awakening at the hour he wished, his senses alert to danger. He was an hour ahead of them, at least. He would need this rest he was going to get. What lay ahead would take everything he had. He knew that.

Their feet would be punishing them cruelly now. Three of them still had their horses, leading them.

He rested his full hour, then got up. He had cut it very thin. Through a space in the rocks, he could see them, not 300 yards away. Lopez, as he had suspected, was in the lead. How easy to pick them off now. But no, he would not kill again. Let their own anxiety to kill him kill them.

Within 100 yards, he had put two jumbled piles of boulders between himself and his pursuers. A little farther then, and he stopped.

Before him was a steep slide of shale, near the edge of a great basin. Standing where he did, he could see, far away in the distance, a purple haze over the mountains. Between there was nothing but a great white expanse, shimmering with heat.

He slid down the shale and brought up at the bottom. He was now, he knew, seventy feet below sea level. He started away, and, at every step, dry, powdery dust lifted in clouds. It caked in his nostrils, filmed his eyelashes, and covered his clothes with whitish, alkaline dust. Far across the Sink, and scarcely discernible from the crest behind him, was the Window in the Rock. He headed for it, walking steadily. It was ten miles if you walked straight across.

So far that Navajo was right, Shad told himself. *And he said to make it before dark . . . or else!*

Shad Marone's lips were dry and cracked. After a mile, he stopped, tilting his canteen until he could get his finger into the water, then carefully moistened his lips. Just a drop then, inside his mouth.

All these men were desert wise. None of them, excepting perhaps Lopez, would know about the Sink. They would need water. They would have to know where to find it. By day they could follow his trail, but after darkness fell . . . ?

And then, the Navajo had said, the wind would begin to blow. Shad looked at the dry, powdery stuff under him. He could imagine what a smothering, stifling horror this would be if the wind blew. Then, no man could live.

Heat waves danced a queer rigadoon across the lower sky, and heat lifted, beating against his face from the hot white dust beneath his feet. Always it was over a man's boot tops, sometimes almost knee deep. Far away, the mountains were a purple line that seemed to waver vaguely in the afternoon sun. He walked on, heading by instinct rather than sight for the Window.

Dust arose in a slow, choking cloud. It came up from his feet in little puffs, like white smoke. He stumbled, then got his feet right, and kept on.

Walking in this was like dragging yourself through heavy mud. The dust pulled at his feet. His pace was slow.

Thirst gathered in his throat, and his mouth seemed filled with something thick and clotted. His tongue was swollen, his lips cracked and swollen. He could not seem to swallow.

He could not make three miles an hour. Darkness would reach him before he made the other side. But he would be close. Close enough. Luckily, at this season, the light stayed long in the sky.

After a long time, he stopped and looked back. Yes, they were coming. But there was not one dust cloud. There were several. Through red-rimmed, sun-squinted eyes, he watched. They were straggling. Every straggler would die. He knew that. Well, they had asked for it.

Dust covered his clothing, and only his gun he kept clean. Every half hour he stopped and wiped it as clean as he could. Twice he pulled a knotted string through the barrel.

Finally he used the last of his water. Every half hour he had been wetting his lips. He did not throw the canteen away, but slung it back upon his hip. He would need it later, when he got to the Nest. His feet felt very heavy, his legs seemed to belong to an automaton. Head down, he slogged wearily on. In an hour he made two miles.

II

There is a time when human nature seems able to stand no more. There is a time when every iota of strength seems burned away. This was the fourth day of the chase. Four days without a hot meal, four days of riding, walking, running. Now this. He had only to stop, they would come up with him, and it would be over.

The thought of how easy it would be to quit came to him. He considered the thought. But he did not consider quitting. He could no more have stopped than a bee could stop making honey. Life was ahead, and he had to live. It was a matter only of survival now. The man with the greatest urge to live would be the one to survive.

Those men behind him were going to die. They were going to die for three reasons. First, he alone knew where there was water, and at the right time he would lose them.

Second, he was in the lead, and after dark they would have no trail, and, if they lived through the night, there would be no trail left in the morning.

Third, at night, at this season, the wind always blew, and their eyes and mouths and ears would fill with soft, white filmy dust, and, if they lay down, they would be buried by the sifting, swirling dust.

They would die then, every man jack of them.

They had it coming. Bowman deserved it. So did

Davis and Gardner. Lopez most of all. They were all there; he had seen them. Lopez was a killer. The man's father had been Spanish and Irish, his mother an Apache.

Without Lopez, he would have shaken them off long before. Shad Marone tried to laugh, but the sound was only a choking grunt. Well, they had followed Lopez to their deaths, all of them. Aside from Lopez, they were weak sisters.

He looked back again. He was gaining on them now. The first dust cloud was farther behind, and the distance between the others was growing wider. It was a shame Lopez had to die, at that. The man was tough and had plenty of trail savvy.

Shad Marone moved on. From somewhere within him he called forth a new burst of strength. His eyes watched the sun. While there was light, they had a chance. What would they think in Puerto de Luna when eight men did not come back?

Marone looked at the sun, and it was low, scarcely above the purple mountains. They seemed close now. He lengthened his stride again. The Navajo had told him how his people once had been pursued by Apaches, and had led the whole Apache war party into the Sink. There they had been caught by darkness, and none was ever seen again according to the Indian's story.

Shad stumbled then and fell. Dust lifted thickly about him, clogging his nostrils. Slowly, like a groggy fighter, he got his knees under him and, using his rifle for a staff, pushed himself to his feet.

He started on, driven by some blind, brute desire for life. When he fell again, he could feel rocks under his hands. He pulled himself up.

He climbed the steep, winding path toward the Window in the Rock. Below the far corner of the Window was the Nest. And in the Nest, there was water. Or so the Navajo had told him.

When he was halfway up the trail, he turned and looked back over the Sink. Far away, he could see the dust clouds. Four of them. One larger than the others. Probably there were two men together.

"Still coming," he muttered grimly, "and Lopez leading them!"

Lopez, damn his soul!

The little devil had guts, though; you had to give him that. Suddenly Marone found himself almost wishing Lopez would win through. The man was like a wolf. A killer wolf. But he had guts. And it wasn't just the honest men who had built up this country to what it was today.

Maybe, without the killers and rustlers and badmen, the West would never have been won so soon. Shad Marone remembered some of them: wild, dangerous men, who went into country where nobody else dared venture. They killed and robbed to live, but they stayed there.

It took iron men for that: men like Lopez, who was a mongrel of the Santa Fé Trail. Lopez had drunk water from a buffalo track many a time. *Well, so have I,* Shad told himself.

Shad Marone took out his six-shooter and wiped it free of dust. Only then did he start up the trail.

He found the Nest, a hollow among the rocks, sheltered from the wind. The Window loomed above him now, immense, gigantic. Shad stumbled, running, into the Nest. He dropped his rifle and lunged for the water hole, throwing himself on the ground to drink. Then he stared, unbelieving.

Empty!

The earth was dry and parched where the water had been, but only cracked earth remained.

He couldn't believe it. It couldn't be! It couldn't . . . ! Marone came to his feet, glaring wildly about. His eyes were red rimmed, his face heat flushed above the black whiskers, now filmed with gray dust.

He tried to laugh. Lopez dying down below there, he dying up here! The hard men of the West, the tough men! He sneered at himself. Both of them now would die, he at the water hole, Lopez down there in the cloying, clogging dust!

He shook his head. Through the flame-sheathed torment of his brain, there came a cool ray of sanity.

There had been water here. The Indian had been right. The cracked earth showed that. But where?

Perhaps a dry season. . . . But, no, it had not been a dry season. Certainly no dryer than any other year at this time.

He stared across the place where the pool had been. Rocks and a few rock cedar and some heaped-up rocks from a small slide. He stumbled across and

216

began clawing at the rocks, pulling, tearing. Suddenly, a trickle of water burst through! He got hold of one big rock and in a mad frenzy tore it from its place. The water shot through then, so suddenly he was knocked to his knees.

He scrambled out of the depression, splashing in the water. Then, lying on his face, he drank, long and greedily.

Finally he rolled away and lay still, panting. Dimly he was conscious of the wind blowing. He crawled to the water again and bathed his face, washing away the dirt and grime. Then, careful as always, he filled his canteen from the fresh water bubbling up from the spring.

If he only had some coffee. . . . But he'd left his food in his saddlebags.

Well, Madge would be all right now. He could go back to her. After this, they wouldn't bother him. He would take her away. They would go to the Blue Mountains in Oregon. He had always liked that country.

The wind was blowing more heavily now, and he could smell the dust. That Navajo hadn't lied. It would be hell down in the Sink. He was above it now and almost a mile away.

He stared down into the darkness, wondering how far Lopez had been able to get. The others didn't matter; they were weak sisters who lived on the strength of better men. If they didn't die there, they would die elsewhere, and the West could spare them. He got to his feet.

Lopez would hate to die. The ranch he had built so carefully in a piece of the wildest, roughest country was going well. It took a man with guts to settle where he had and make it pay. Shad Marone rubbed the stubble on his jaw. *That last thirty head of his cows I rustled for him brought the best price I ever got!* he remembered thoughtfully. *Too bad there ain't more like him!*

Well, after this night, there would be one less. There wouldn't be anything to guide Lopez down there now. A man caught in a thick whirlpool of dust would have no landmarks; there would be nothing to get him out except blind instinct. The Navajos had been clever, leading the Apaches into a trap like that. Odd, that Lopez's mother had been an Apache, too.

Just the same, Marone thought, he had nerve. He'd shot his way up from the bottom until he had one of the best ranches.

Shad Marone began to pick up some dead cedar. He gathered some needles for kindling and in a few minutes had a fire going.

Marone took another drink. Somehow he felt restless. He got up and walked to the edge of the Nest. How far had Lopez come? Suppose. . . . Marone gripped his pistol.

Suddenly he started down the mountain. "The hell with it," he muttered.

A stone rattled.

Shad Marone froze, gun in hand.

Lopez, a gray shadow, weaving in the vague light

from the cliff, had a gun in his hand. For a full minute, they stared at each other.

Marone spoke first. "Looks like a dead heat," he said.

Lopez said: "How'd you know about that water hole?"

"Navajo told me," Shad replied, watching Lopez like a cat. "You don't look so bad," he added. "Have a full canteen?"

"No. I'd have been a goner. But my mother was an Apache. A bunch of them got caught in the Sink once. That never happened twice to no Apache. They found this water hole then, and one down below. I made the one below, an' then I was finished. She was a dry hole. But then water began to run in from a crack in the rock."

"Yeah?" Marone looked at him again. "You got any coffee?"

"Sure."

"Well," Shad said as he holstered his gun, "I've got a fire."

About the Editor

Jon Tuska is the author of numerous books about the American West as well as editor of several short story collections, *Billy the Kid: His Life and Legend* (Greenwood Press, 1994) and *The Western Story: A Chronological Treasury* (University of Nebraska Press, 1995) among them. Together with his wife Vicki Piekarski, Tuska co-founded Golden West Literary Agency that primarily represents authors of Western fiction and Western Americana. They edit and co-publish twenty-five titles a year in two prestigious series of new hardcover Western novels and story collections, the Five Star Westerns and the Circle Ⓥ Westerns. They also co-edited the *Encyclopedia of Frontier and Western Fiction* (McGraw-Hill, 1983), *The Max Brand Companion* (Greenwood Press, 1996), *The Morrow Anthology of Great Western Short Stories* (Morrow, 1997), and *The First Five Star Western Corral* (Five Star Westerns, 2000). Tuska has also edited a series of short novel collections, *Stories of the Golden West*, of which there have been seven volumes.

Center Point Publishing
600 Brooks Road ● PO Box 1
Thorndike ME 04986-0001 USA

(207) 568-3717

US & Canada:
1 800 929-9108
www.centerpointlargeprint.com

LP   8/07
W/LAM   29.95
L'Amour, Louis
Law of the desert

DATE DUE

OC 0 1 0			
OC 1 0 7			
OC 2 5 0			
NO0 7 0			
ND2 8 0			
DE 1 7 0			
JA 2 5 0			
MR3 1 0			
NO 0 4 0			
NO 0 4 1			
DE 27 '1			
MY 1 8 '1			

DISCARD

DEMCO